JaMes PeTer BasTiEn

SÈ LAVI DE MOI: ~ BY 9 INITIATIVE

I am life from the essence of birth. Though I have not experience life thru the existing of death but thru birth only, I only live around a surrounding which fears death. I am time in effect too my causes, I learn more by mind then threw body, the body can only be at one place where as the mind can travel by the seconds. A jack too my nothing, a master of all. I know nothing but all, all but nothing. JaMes BasTiEn is an Melanin Man with ancestral background of an Afrikan bloodline traced from the Levite tribe, one of twelve from Judah. Location is set from Yoruba, Benin, a town in West of Nigeria, this placed me forward to a land known prior as Saint-Dominigue, later changed to Ayiti, the land of mountains where the biggest slave revolt was established by the effort for change. From where the name was executed to define the people and of there wrong doings, the land of hate, those who hate themselves became known to the world as Haiti. I'm now feeling the effect of an eastern mind with my body being in the west. Hemispheres have energies and spirits that have significant similarities but different by values. An Author, Athlete, Musician, Actor, Entertainer, my biggest gift too the universe is creating. I create on the aspect of things that can enhance our experience universally, if cannot assist for the better, I simply respect this for what its for. I do not build to destroy, the actions of my opposition. Celf Love, Best Love. Let's create, World Love.

Introduction:

Warning, I advise any reader who comes across, before picking up this bare truth, understand some pain will be felt internally, as any truth, no lie, although we're living the truth in lies. Non external pain as this will possess some mental views, feelings, and conscious decisions that will showcase me, the Soul of mine, writing as me too thy, from the spectrum of mine, mind. I'm so balance, so in my pain, I'm stronger. I have to be man enough and name a brotha of mines who came into my journey of life, forever if you love this honesty that I will display base on my personal view points, upraising, growth, then I may request you provide that same love for the bredren Malik D. Told me something I already knew, yet afraid to do, then I processed and listened, "voila" this became true. Self I will spell as Celf. Reasoning, I would say is my understanding of cells being millions of different particles working as one unit. Definitely not the scientific definition, I can bet that's certain I'm wrong by definition of cells but my direct response to that is life is in the eye of the beholder, I see my celf as millions of pieces unified by the flesh which is hidden within my spirit and mind. We all know, we don't live the same, in the same home, different countries, but manure however smells the same. Something about nature made just think!, "Nothing is different if at the end of the stick, it's only opposite. I mean , is opposite different when unity is the middle ground between both parties !?" . You've just been mind .... . I'm actually smarter then appear and that's what hurts me because I can't say the precise reasoning that I'm here. Feeling short, midget Mack, lemme get a beer. Clearly I have an bound with words that gravitates to poetry, setting the next move, can't skip a beat, that's moetry. I get it, not a word, just a joke, you know, " If lady motion and mister poetry had a baby, the baby would be !?", laugh out loud for reals, I laugh writing, your opinions keep it to yourself. So I've been debating if I should curse in this writing material. Internally I feel not to, externally I feel fake not being direct to my speech in certain decisions that I would normally utilize. "Decisions, decision's, So the saying goes. I'll prevail to not curse, Reasoning, my truth shouldn't be limited to anyone, young, old, middle age should have no issues reading this material, this is simply my truths. I want to make sure it's either artistry I'm articulating threw my word play, or feelings and understandings that I've learned and gained that's being displayed from experiences, education, and surroundings. That's gains threw pain in my eyes summit as truths. Truth I cannot give you from the perspective of life, nature, humanity, religion, sex, and cultures. Those I'm sure you want an definite answer, I'm aware, I'm not the preacher that's gonna sell you on hope, faith, wish nor believe. Never been my feng shui, gonna get the truth raw and sometimes dirty. Surely my upraising was the reasoning behind such statements as I realize all adults are big kids with less rules and boundaries. My upraising of getting an onion instead of an lemon too create lemonade gave me a love for the truth that was an bound to be. The hardship of my adolescence gave me an ownership take of my own livelihood that I would of not been able to process nor view if was just an child as an kid. Hurts too admit too any mother how babying the baby can lead weak dependence adult life's effecting mentally, physically, spiritually, since we in the modern era, the fourth plane of this weak dependency has become finance or has such always been !?. The "Googoo Gaagaa", "I want toys, just be a kid, let me handle your bills, go to school", foreign conversations I've yet to encounter. "First stage of getting better or over in anything is ?". That's right , you got it, I know you would of got it. That's another laugh out loud for me. I'm an tad bit hilarious which match my seriousness in demeanor at times. I'm looking to keep you awake, feeling you with pleasantry while taking direct bullets to the heart every sentences. Not literal of course, in writing, I disclaim. Must you be safe these days, "sensitivity", " he threatened me in writing form, yes !, threw a book you honor !". I'm so hilarious, now reread that quote and think of an image of the person you feel would fit that quote the best........ 9, let me not be judge mental, happens too me to much to not know "the grass ain't greener" theory. Polarity, I speak such, because I'm living such. You thought I forgot didn't ya, the first stage of getting better at or over anything is admitting !, you had it from jump, this will mean the get go, from the beginning, By duality which made my decision not to curse is the same polarity life which aide me to write in the proper grammar at times while some expressions takes a different approach as I am bilingual speaking creole as my first language followed by English. Between both language I carry multiple vocal and visual dialects which you have in creole the proper (class) and country (non class), So they say. English, I have an mixture of an intellect blend with what would be called in proper dictionary terms "ghetto", "hood", or "southern". I'm an intellect base on me being an nerd too understanding which forces me to learn what people, places, and things mean or define as. My upraising base on words, communication, understanding was definitely the non class country folk from Ayiti mix with the ghetto southern English Broward County raised Zoe, as they say. By the way, let's blink and think. Who art thou is they ?. "The man", I can hear and see a brotha side wavering his neck, eyes rolled back, " so you gon act stupid, the man brotha". Just saying, I don't take his story as my truth, sorry I meant history. What is mirrored as someone else perspective is not my truth. Remember, separates the difference between inner & outer, the soul & flesh, mind & body, however you wanna interpret. I'm big on "lessons over actions", in lots of time, we feel we as humans, we can control the outcome way more than we think we can learn from anything that actually occurs. I've learned from my perspective by knowledge and experience truth, meaning "my truth in experience but however may work or not work for you", perspective truth. I've learned that I learn way more after I've experience someone or something, I knew now way more now then I that I knew of thee experience before hand. Feelings and emotions can aide you at times but certainly can degrade you to what actually can be definite or truthful. I would say the closes anyone can get to learn before experience would be using logic. Logic I perceive is my spirit from the meaning " using your two senses". Logic I perceive to be the marriage between the spirit and the flesh. Being logical, the gray area, I can admit that I can see from being logical brings some tough decisions which will leave you and or your surroundings hurtful or not on good terms base on the decisions you made or make. I know this due to the fact that being logical has A lot of narcissistic characteristics. The inner voice that speaks too you, what's stronger too you, the outer voices or the inner ?. This effect has nothing to do with being intellect or non witty, this is simply how we humans are created, baby narcissist, funny how we share life on earth but in you lives a universe. No scientific explanation, religion, or another person can tell you how you feel better then you can. The body, mind and souls have there own feelings and expressions. Can you assume correctly ?, yes, can you make an glute cheek out of yourself, I don't see why not, why of course you can. The reasoning I feel assumptions can guess correctly is that the body is the middle between all three entities which controls you internally. The spirit, flesh, and mind the next person carries as you. As you can only assume threw the body and see someone wickedness base on anger, someone else may see pain, someone else may see hurt, another fear and so on. What you can read out from an person spirit or what's in there mind far as intellect is only by signs or Ora that the body can give out from what's within. Telepathy I've read and comply to understand to be if ever was the first language, if truly language break downs to connecting threw connections. The idea of using are eyes, hands, nose, mouths, feet, sounds, nature and many more options as a way to communicate seems just about right that telepathy first stood grounds. Then language came along and said " I have a dream, that one day will all be separated by the forces invested by thy " differences govern by choices", having humanity pick on one another until I see dead flies everywhere". That language fool is no joke, do you hear me?. Very probable you can hear me because your mind has a voice when you read me that's make out a of voice within you while reading this art in writing illustration. So I will not be doing an audio book. Celf reflection states the experience for your understanding is better if I leave this for only as an reading material rather than audio or visual. Of course it will be easier for you threw audio and video, but I rather train you too use your powers, not to store them away and forgetting your abilities like I was, or they thought I would. They put to *rest, "my birth parents who wanted me to fail", they is an excuse to talk, I have no excuses, I only have a reason to speak. I'm direct. No chain elephants in my sermons, I aim to free minds and uplift spirits. I need your attention with eyes with these words but your visions and voice, I owe you the favor to not take away your powers of imagination, epiphany, and most importantly your perspective on what you feel. As life becomes easier socially and with location securement, we but all forget the privacy and own powers we're giving up for what's already an robotic assembly line monitored life. This is my story, I certainly was not born by an river next to an border fence, though my river eyes been running every sense, its been a painful pleasure being me. Thank you again my brotha Malik, I needed this continuation of what's free for me, be honest and direct, beneficiate all sounds soulfully, BASS. My brotha is my brotha although is he's not my mothers kid, I'm vice versa. I close this introduction with, I have more names that I can drop that will take an chapter to express or give times in appreciation too. Chob, I owe you one brotha, I Love you my brotha, whatever that one is, if you need, forever gotcha thy brotha. What's explain don't need to be understood, this here only for those who could. When I think about what I'm writing, this is clear thought writing, this is me, no pressure, as nervous i am to be out there about me, I'm so anxious to deliver me. I know I'm very dual, sun and moon as I explain earlier. My mind is exploding with so many to give you that I have to be honest with myself and decide how I'm going to deliver my experiences threw words being transparent as possible, opening your eyes but not describing an* story about a house and taking ten minutes just to open the front door base on descriptive depth writing. My reasoning to not curse, where I know my future seeds or any child can be mines, goes my reasoning to express all my dialects in upraising that I can affirm internally. I'm here to educate, progress life, never decreasing. I know from the bottom of my heart, I can forgive, I've had. Forgiving myself for what I've been threw is tough. Taking responsibility is an requirement for me that keeps Celf grounded as being my own parent and my own creative director of effects since thirteen. I say 13 because I remember the financial shift my life took, earlier than, life was tougher because my dependency led to others one hunnid percent lacking assistance, excuse thy, one hundred percent. Certainly was not easy but the sense of pride being independent brought to me the " Ha ha, you can't tell Nathan" feeling was worth living every-time. Which, some great came out from, taking ownership, and a lot of bad, not having an support system and making poor decisions along the way. I see violets as red and roses sing blues, my flesh is ahead, in spirit one livid thy trues........9

Initiative 1:

~1 of 1

September 26, 1989.

What time was my birth ?, "ask Islaine, yet to inform me". Where was the location ?, "Plantation FL". "Do I know my father ?", "of course, met him at the age of 26". What day was I born " On a Tuesday, yea that's lady night at the club, sorry mama, I would of prefer Sunday, I feel I am an sun baby". What else does a biography ask ?, oh of course my birth giver name is Islaine Pierre by which was switched when I was I believe twelve or thirteen marrying who became an great father figure and role model, great man, Levelt Corneille. The seed giver to my mothers garden for my birth was Lucien Bastien. Having no relations with my biological father until the age of 26 left me mentally alienated of course for many reasonings but I hold no deeper pain from his absence no lesser or greater than my birth giver celf hate to not love her Celf enough where she hated all that she created. I'm one of three from my birth giver womb, and one of two from my seed giver doings, so he said prior. Most I recalled from repetitive thoughts early in time was being an child and wondering "is anybody gonna take ownership for me ?, did I birth myself, hello, parents of my world, you had sex, had a child, I'm the cause too you two effects, you know, a little assistance from my flesh creators would sure help a lot to grow big and strong,". Another saying, " eat your fruits and vegetables so you can grow up big and strong". Yes, "can't wait to bite into those chemicals preservatives you've applied", not nature's doing but yours. I'm direct so you is gonna be either the "Secret Societies", "Governments", "GMO farming", etc, our food crisis base on dietary is next too global warming, deadly if you actually comprehend what food is. There's a lot of saying in this Western Hemisphere , or precisely the earth we dwell in. Why do we take others quoting as answers for us?, "Well i feel, I think, I see". Shh, you can be quiet if you like now, you are appreciated now "thaaaanks". That wasn't rude was it ?. Everybody has an opinion about an action they would not do. So yes, my inner voice was my first parent, senses keeping me alive, eyes allowing me to view the world by surroundings, my nose that's gives out positive or negative smells like energy, ears that I used like a sponge to soak up words and each comprehension of meaning. The experience of Ayiti Also known as Haiti, being me, I'm an analytical nerd. Etymology states Haiti is define as the land of hate, curses is an Haitian who would be the "one whose born in hate", "those who hate themselves". I found it funny which why in English writing was the named changed followed by the spelling. With any other country, America would change the spelling for pronunciation purposes but not alter the full naming of such country. As Brasìl is changed to Brazil, Cúba as Cuba and many other South American and Caribbean countries pronunciation changes but not the actual name. To say Ayiti too Haiti is the same means I'm walking around with bulges of screws loose in my head and hearing my keys jingle means I'm intelligent. Options if I may offer, "Ayete", "Ahiti",

"Aeyeti", let's just be honest, that's a little off if we gonna say it's for pronunciation purposes, but way closer to the word hate, Haiti. When's there lie, you can always expect a bull, relaxing while manuring on your lawn, your lawn being your mind, Marinated. Saved me with love, My grandmother raised me until I was eight years old. I can never forget that day when my uncle Jean pack me up leaving Port Dé Paix transferring to Port Au Prince by bus on the pursuit of catching a flight to where he said was my home. He just said Miami I was heading too. Funny thing is, for most Ayisens, Florida is America , New York is in Florida just as Miami and Boston. So yea, geographic is not a primary study in Ayiti, also I may disclaim this was coming from an country boy perspective of what we knew. I remember him being so excited for me and rubbing my head " Ou prale Miami negum, ou bon", you're going to Miami, you're fine. Little did he know, I was piss like a mug. Brotha, I'm leaving my grandmother, my auntie Leonie, My uncles, and you laughing, I remember thinking, dude is cold hearted, my world is tearing apart and you're excited for my departure ?. Who I knew and develop to be my mother since six 6 months old as was written to be, felt like my umbilical cord being detach all over again from an first experience I never can feel existed before. Wait, what ?, I thought you said you were born in plantation FL, how you get to Ayiti at six months old, fluctuation in delegations, my story is unstably stable. I'm thirty now, I promise I would not even been able to tell you this how or when five years ago. If you'd met me before I was 9, I would of gave you the incorrect birth date too my own, month I had correctly but that's a

funny story I'll share with you in regards to how I learned my actual birthdate, be prepare, hilarious too some, some tears may fall for those with encounter experiences. Be a soldier if you gonna cry, let your hand take some healing water from your emotions and wipe those tears when needed, no tissues nor napkins. How I got too Ayiti, I bound this as my truth of perspective with the three months I spent with my father in Jonesboro GA. Unfortunately for me, between my mother unapproachable ways and her side of family backing up such manner, I knew nothing about my father, no pictures of him until days before turning 26, no baby pictures, or the why too my name. Whole lotta nada like enchilada, not any stories of my own he's stories giving back to me from my mother side. In Ayiti, I grew to think that I was sent there because she couldn't take care of me back in the U.S and had to work a lot was too my reasoning for being sent. This also being the norm for a lot of other islanders sending there kids to go live back home for many situations, just as my reasoning was bad, are some good reasons another mother or father can send there child. I remember having that resentment like I don't know my father at all, yet my mother doesn't want me, but I'm with my grandma, sucks, ahh, but who cares. Until I was called back to the U.S.. A sad day that came with more opportunities but at the same time hardship I could of ever imagine would be flowing with wings with me. There's three side to every story so I'll do my best to not let it be one sided. Though Islaine never admitted too sending me to Ayiti for malicious reasoning or speak on such matter ever, her actions once I arrived was Golden to what was explained from Lucien. From what I was told, They we're together for a year or two, living there life's, him managing his businesses, from what i here this is true after my aunties and uncles confirmed such after knowing me my whole life and couldn't tell me one thing about the guy. I had to get it straight from the horses mouth for information on my own life, so I did. Yes living there life came with some battles, I have to be honest and say when somebody provide you an story and give you there wrongfulness or what led them to misjudge a situation or be uncertain, that's a grain a salt that can season a whole pot. Most when at wrong, hide there fault, so you get the truth of lies, my truths from my lying perspective. The guy spoke to me as an men, so I had to respect it. From being honest about it was a sexual compatibility then to lie and say "it was spiritual, mental". From his honesty of verbal abuse, I'm sure if it was some physical due to him being the reason Islaine hated me or the excuse she gives her celf for the celf hate. Islaine from when I seen visited Ayiti when I was about five or six years old . She was light caramel skinned voluptuous lady with curves, the seek of most men attention, that's my birth giver but I know now, being an grown man, ain't too much men at the time who probably did not want to be with her in some sort of fashion. Lucien, did also states he was talking too one her family member before they started talking which I'll remain nameless out of celf respect. Stated this family member acted for bigger fishes in south Florida's early cocaine drug dealing era and did not take him serious base on finance at the time and introduced Lucien to Islaine who later became a couple. He stated he caught her cheating multiple times and although he did, she did not ever catch him red headed as she's been, she knew he cheated but he did not care she knew, it was like an eye for eye mentality, a child's game played between two grown big kids. Threw it all, I'm not sure if they was ever in love or was it the simple common fashion of relationships for needs, wants, and desires. You learn more in experiencing, relationships are base on status, worth's, abilities then the simple reasoning of love by mutuality. It's an complicated world, I truly have one choice that should always be mines and that's the person I chose to be with. As you know, my seeds givers knows, your parents and I know, the pendulum on the pole does not always swing to side you'll like such too. I recall questioning him at once, " if you two had all these problems before, why in the world did yawl decide to have an child?". So he told me, he told the story of an man thinking with his penis and an womban using her vagina as fish bait to create Bass, catch up no ketchup. Touchdown, born me out of an Hail Mary pass. She cheated, he's paying all bills, threats of you got to leave, desperation's she pleads, "let's have an baby". He wanted too have kids with Islaine but said she still wanted to party and live a fun life, so that left him nervous. Islaine knew want he wanted, Lucien, desperate times calls for desperate measures. She took his life source and he took her body. Perhaps I was conceived December 25, 1988, my cousins Gary birthday, who may have been conceived March 24, 1988, another of my cousins, Nick birthday. Exactly nine months apart is all three of us. Always I weirdly think if he's story is an lie amongst what happened, then maybe

I would just made from an wombman intuition with having baby fever. This made me thought, couples, especially I would say the wombman baby fever is off the roof once a family or friend gives birth, a frenzy to have is established. In that regards, I was born 9.26.89. My understanding from Lucien, after three months of my birth, Islaine left him. Empty apartment with just a microwave with his son gone was the home he walked into after twelve hours ago, he's home was furnished with his lady and child present. Reasoning he stated, money in the cleaning businesses was down And the extracurricular activities for an young in her twenties female was not gonna work if she was to be with an older male. I know he's over an decade older then her but like my statement about relationships, wants, needs, desires will make pretend happiness and playing a double life sounds just about normal and acceptable. His point from here was to get life on track as he told his side, he was not doing right in Florida financially to which he decided to make a move to Georgia for an New opportunity. Troubling grounds between Lucien and Islaine did not lesser as he advised she refused to allow him to see me and order him to either pay up or don't show up. Again thus far, all my perspective from zero days old to about two years old are better known by my surroundings then I can actually say why this or that occurred. He goes to say he moved to Georgia about when I was four months asking to split custody, access denied by boss lady, no Bueno. So he then said after two or three trips coming for the weekend back and forth from GA to FL, though she did not give him access, he knew at the time the home of her friend who babysit me while Islaine was at work and would let him play and stay with me before she come picks me up from work. States on the second or third trip, he was advised by that same person, I was sent to Ayiti. Being that his name was on my birth certificate, he had the right to give consent of yes or no to send me on an plane as a infant and she could not send me too another country without no mutual agreement. Then he goes on to tell me, she had two options, either have me returned ASAP or he could of had Islaine deported and have her visa revoked for doing such act, I cannot tell if what he said is factual or not, again this is the one side I've ever gotten to hear. As an result to his demand, he advise me that he later came to find out that the situation was more complicated then what he thought. The truth was that I was not sent to Ayiti on an vacation but rather on an permanent stay. What stated too have occurred was, in the Caribbean islands, like the kids being sent back to be raised there, this is normal where people utilize different names or change there identity for an opportunity of coming too the U.S.. Truthfully admitting this does not mean, these our "evil wicked people", for the better, you'll do a lot if you've never had. In that regards once I reached too the island, My papers far as passport, birth certificate and social was sold to another father who had an infant he was looking to bring to the states. Who sold my papers !?, only one party confirm this, which is Lucien. Islaine never spoke of. Threw the great vine, I've heard this act was assisted by Islaine uncle who was known for doing such work in this field of identity hustling, theft. So back to the lawyers and deportation situation. Speaking to her family, Lucien said he did not want her to be deported so he backed off and gave an alternative which in six months must I be return or else he's to call the shot for her deportation. In this process he advised the truth was to be reveal sooner than later, he finally got the truth out of her uncle and the issue was that they couldn't have me return because of this fact. JaMes BasTiEn already has been reported to be back in the U.S days after I initially went, someone else was under my alias as I was in Ayiti. He then was a man to me and said he left it alone. That was hurtful, to learn your father didn't put in that extra fight for you but it was a gift for him not to sugar honey ice tea me, no sugarcoated answer. Never been a vegan, told you I get it and like it raw, no pun intended, just direct. Complication, as man cannot carry life in womb nor give birth, this experience helps me see why this becomes so easy for me to detach emotionally naturally. Men don't like complication, if it's too hard, we rather restart over and get a fresh beginning. My opinion, it's easier to be intrigued on what we haven't experienced then to be loyal to what we know, The whole from cave men to explorer theory. I realize after playing me out for a business deal three months after getting to know my seed giver, I learned that every men is not the same and you cannot judge wisdom by age. I may have never been or have been threw more things then Lucien. I over stand I think way better with my penis then he'll ever be after this dude was still into buying wombman love base off what he can get from them. Sounds childish right, remember adults are just fully developed big kids. I was told, "please my son, if I died tomorrow, at least you can come take this house in Georgia". Lies, there's twenty nine years mortgage left on this house, this is not yours buddy. "I have three cars, you can go to school and be alright", another lie, "I'm gonna take $10,000 out my pension and we start a business", you smart and heard it all before, I'm not into repeating self. Eventually after the three months of lies, was tough financially but artistically, I got more info on his upraising, Mom, I remembering him in my head saying "Marie" but I could be wrong, his Father name "Cheri" for sure. I remembered because of so many talks about his dad. Ironic for me, that's always the ideal name I had for my first born daughter, Cheri "sweetheart" in Creole. More he gave on his sisters, friends, exes, had to respect that . An open dialect that I've never ever gotten in the twenty six years of my life. I appreciated his lies because the opposite was the truth that he wanted me there. Or did he ?. Before leaving Georgia to head back too Florida, I end up opening an real estate investment company as begun researching how to flip houses. Did not have money to invest upfront, I've then learned about abandoned houses and the process on how to take ownership for, far as being an written landlord to rent out too tenants. I ended up having an apartment ready set in motion back in Fort Lauderdale that my cousin was living in but moved out of and provided me the owners information. The plan was too get a stable job and create on the side as an artist and businessman. Between Lucien not capable of paying his mortgage after leasing a new truck and me not being able to go school due to only one car made the decision to move back too Florida super easy. Weeks became months of researching gave me the ideas of contracting the real *estate company as the landlord for Lucien mortgaged home. Essentially he paid under $500 a month for his mortgage in which I ended up renting to a family profiting $1,000 after taking monthly mortgage out owed to the bank. This was considered to be an 50/50 deal with him and I, the deposit $4,000, same situation, 50/50. As his always been into handymen man work as an landscaper and mechanical work, we were able to save by working as direct resources to our own real estate investment company. Due to yarding, fencing, and painting an out of date abandoned duplex, We ended up getting landlord controlled with the proof work to the bank which did request Lucien a $2,000 down payment to take ownership as the landlord. Not that easy as written, essence is time so filing paper work is an essence of patience. $1500 deposit was required for the move in, and $750 was our price per apartment as two total the duplex as one. $300 was to go back to the bank as property owner. Got one out of two filled up. This is two days before I leave Georgia for Florida, Taking care of paperwork, running backgrounds, drawing out the terms of contracts. Like I told him, "I appreciate you taking ownership as a man, I'm not gonna shun you for what you cannot do for me or what you've told me you had prior, let's build an empire NOW". I'd never heard we or lived with Anyone with the same last name as me, I was just proud to create with my pops I thought. Trust is for suckers, I trust that humans are gonna be humans, so if I can trust your not perfect, why put a trust that you will do something for me which takes perfection from your time given. I trusted him, apartment ready for me to move in back in*

Lauderhill, FL. My ex and I at the time thinking we finally get to build, so much of our love was base on hardship and determination but no stability with security given I felt by me. Just hours, upon awaiting for Lucien to get off from work and western Union my money, $2700 in deposit for both location, he tells me he can't today because he's gonna have to move all his stuff out the house while moving in his new rented apartment. Understandable, this was Thursday, "Friday, after work you'll be getting this", he stated Thursday. Friday, like if he was four hours late on his shift, I called him repetitively, yet still was he was a no call, no show. Saturday I'm on edge, "my blood seed giver did not just play me" is all I'm thinking. Sunday, got the automatic voicemail. Monday I played a character, an concern son who have not heard from his dad since he moved back four days ago, manager panics and runs with phone, " Lucien, Lucien, your son said he haven't heard from you since four days ago , his worried". A back noise responded, "tell him I call him later". Later came, got the call, "my phone fell in water, I couldn't call you my Son". Silence from me then I laughed like, "sir I'm homeless waiting on this funds". He responded," that's all you wanted from huh, your mother side of the family are just money bandits, I should of known that's why you came too Georgia". Click goes the phone, I stare up as my head rest in the car seat, thinking, "what just happened", laughing, "this can't be real", thinking, "don't get angry, play smart, apologize if that's what he wanna hear, just call back, keep your cool, get that CTN number". Got voicemail over all my attempts for the next three days until he said I'll just change my number.

Don't trust the eyes for all seen and think, takes a second to trust but a change in an blink. Shall we continue 9........

Initiative 2 :

~ Simplicity

Life was simple in Ayiti, no lights for eight months out the year, you eat what you grow, school was daily and year round from what you heard, seen, smelled, or touched. Louisa Pierre, my Goddess, normality was provided from the nurturing and development aspect given by my birth giver mother and intermediate family. The best part I recall being a kid was the lack of worries and appreciation for simplicity. I cared too eat, play, sleep, play, play, eat, sleep. This was all of us at one point in life, then we separated. Think wherever you are and I'll admit too perceiving, not a direct statement. Any teenager or older can not enjoy and utilize there imaginations better than one whose an teenager or younger. Simplicity is for kids, complications is for adults. The biggest heartbreak I can recall in my time living in Ayiti had to be loosing "Cheri mwen, matant Zan", my auntie Zan died about when I was four or five years old, three to four years after coming back to the U.S. since birth. After giving birth too my baby cousin Stevenson, the baby died after living under six months if not lesser. Hard for me to give you an definite answer. I was a child myself but I remember going with her to clinics and from birth Stevenson having so much medical issues which needed attentive care. Following the baby death was her, yet I was growing still like pain threw gain. The lesson I had to take from this heartbreak was overcoming, many was on the way, I was just being prepped for. Not always true, but at times, the eight year old boy or girl from a "third world country" (lacking foundation, resources, education), maybe more advance mentally and physically base upon what there surroundings asking of them to complete. We're talking smoking already, playing house and pretending to be daddy and mommy's, some live fast because some die young, theory. Not too much you can hide from kids in a third world country, there I was, exposed to reality. Witty, capable, intrigued are wording I can most certainly say carried with me since knowing how to speak or walk. Exquisitely, I became an chameleon, observer to my beings & an actor to my doings. I did not attend school in Ayiti, education was not and still not free, not just Ayiti, in most if not every place, you pay for education in some sort of fashion. I ended up going for a short period of time. I cannot say if finance was the reason behind me not attending school prior, but the moral of the story is my family paid the price to send me and so did I. There's an old thick oak wood hand carved desk, our classroom stored in a wooden shack builted school. Our class floor is tiled covered under some dirt, big rugs in multiple areas for the teachers chalk boards, desk and our play area. "Mwen ka fe". That's creole for I can do it, under five minutes later that I can do it knocked me out cold to where I recalled last waking up to my mouth being barb wired, a room of concern family members and a sudden pain I could not explained occurred. So much I couldn't recall until months later, my grandmother ran into the mother of the boy who allegedly at the time got me knocked out. I know right, got beat so bad can't remember who did it ?,not quite. Still during this altercation I was confused about the argument my grandmother was having with this lady until my grandmother said in creole " gade sa petite ou fe petite mwen", Look what your child did too mines. At this moment I got it while she grabbed my mouth showing off my missing front teeth, ripped sensitive gums, swollen jaws from having my jawbone misplaced. I could not remember what occurred besides me waking up in pain, I simply remember the rehab off pain and eating out of a straw for a while, not sure how long was this, calendars is never a kid top priority I can assure. My heart hurts sometimes for that kid that was me, the why me factor was the constant feeling. I remember getting older balling my fist when I was mad hoping somebody would test me just to let the anger out for the vulnerable kid that so many picked on or tested wrongfully. I then went to my uncles and explained in details what occured at the market with the kid Mom and Grandma . From what the students and teacher stated, the teacher asked the class to solve an equation that she displayed on board. Raising my hand, "I can do it", she picked me and I begin my walk to the desk. Must of done pretty well, the class cheered as got the equation correctly. I was told that I danced or I'd did a made spin move for celebration. On my way back to my desk, high fives and admiration was given. Not everybody was happy, in your moment of moments, the reaper stands behind looking for objectives that can ascend he or she grin. My smile, I can't recall but was my first realization of jealousy. The way I learn the effects of jealousy was threw me. Celf hate, celf blame, questioning myself so much and thinking "man I wanna get even with this kid". This just the coding layer of the iceberg base on the pain that I really felt. Duality, I was in my early eighteenth or nineteenth years of living. I had to let go despite not wanting too of what had already been done, yet thy felt like I betrayed my own sins of not getting even. How can I ever be, blaming he for what had happen to me. Walking back to my desk proud as can be, by the way, I'm honest and cannot paint you a picture of this kid mind-frame for sticking his leg out to trip me. Walking high and proud, my legs went under like an invisible tree log appeared. For some reason, traumatically, after hearing the story giving from my uncles, my memories cleared up, not too much but just enough to replay the crucial collision in my head over and over, learning at the same time that I can paint a picture or create a film with details given from words. That old thick wooden desk I explained prior was not for your entertainment. This would be my match in colliding full force with. Scared and nervous I panic following this fear with a twirling spin which ended with a mouth open "ahhhhh" straight on contact with that thick oak wood whose still undefeated in all fights brought against. This led to a direct unconscious knocked down by the "Oakwood" desk, your the champ. Explanation by those who were there was giving immediately. After my knockout kids panic, blood gushing mouth was I, teachers and staff ran with me home, to where I would remember waking up. How long was I knocked out?, never found out. Being an observe, would I have laugh at the tripped kid ?. Realizing I would not if it was me made me think, "too laugh at my sorrow is a token coined for an insecure soul". Since I didn't know this kid too have problems with me or I have with him, how can I honestly say this result is what he wanted to happen to me introspectively. Would I done the same if I was in that manner of just wanting to make me trip to embarrass me and get laugh at. Or is it that I can bet on certainty that he was a jealous hater that planned to trip so that I can have my mouth wide open, twirl and bust my mouth open, loosing my fronts in that process, getting knocked out unconscious ? . He planned all that?, must of planned me moving from Broward to Ayiti as well did he. Causes and effects, why is

29

ownership so important !?. Let's find out as life continues each individual moments........9

Initiative 3:

~ Spirit vs Flesh War

I'm not a man of faith, wish, hope, believe, but boy or girl, have I seen such work. I'm thinking, my word play is separated based on direct communication or verbal sarcasm. Some say words are words of the world creator and other planets, stars and universe. Infinity if you mirror those to be the truth. I respect too much to disrespect so much. I put no emphasis on and in our soul creator as I simply don't know but intrigued daily to discover. Me being able to see the religious word play as believe being an example is the truth just as about the same percentage such mirrors a lie. Can the biggest lie or truth teller really, really, really be differentiate ?. Word and bond, law of attraction, prayers, meditations, visioning, acting out, affirmations, different in totality but the same by polarity. As above so below, as below so above. I battled and battled until I finally beat myself then resurrecting my losing celf to beat the winning celf. I was a believer of God, Jesus, Bible, Religion. The Bible God is an jealous God, angered if admire anyone but he, yet he gives you the permission to announce your sins from an another entity as God by following his son, " in the name of Jesus". Upraising, my grandmother feared God in me, not intentionally, just as she knew God to be, tough and righteous since the devil works overtime. Cliche words we may never know the true meaning behind but we say for comfort, at least sounds good too another ear. I wonder what sarcasm sounds like too a fool ?, "ahh", one can only imagine superiority at its highest for this foolish mind. My flight too America was with a family friend so I wouldn't be a minor traveling alone. Before I even made it out of Ayiti, of course remorseful, bittersweet. "I'm about to get on an airplane, hope I don't die !" was my fresh off the boat moment inside Port Au Prince airport . Just the experience of being inside the airport showed me more then I ever saw in my first eight years besides the old movies of America on Television when electricity was given a quarter out of the year. I was thrown off minutes before getting on the plane with this family friend, checking in and seeing the difference in people was all new to me. I heard no other language besides creole in person and English which I perceived was gibberish on Television. From that day, my life changed more than I can imagine. I don't have any specific details about the flight experience, I don't recall. I can always remember getting out of the airport and thinking, creole in my mind of course but "what's wrong with this people, look how they're wasting all these lights". I mean it's one thing too see but I'm squinted from the sparking flashy lights. In opposition of this stick I thought, "AWESOME !". Knowing what I know now, it felt like I was in toy land type of movie my mind viewed the airport as. First step on an escalator, my heart dropped, country boy syndrome. My second step, "I'm moving without walking, where am I", liking something you don't know is like a baby fixating there face to a smell until the taste reach there spectrum by understanding. According to my cousin after checking me out the airport. My birth giver, aunties, and cousin Gary picked me up, where I recall me and him instantly clicking, literally. He then stated, they stopped at Wendy's to get some food where I goes "Wowww, this is where we live!?, why we got so much lights at our house ?". That is hilarious but I think that's his fresh of the boat joke on me he got forever, or maybe I did. If so, I forgive you Bass, you embarrassed me backed then, I forgive you brotha, my flesh is you soul, I'm one in one. The fun ended quickly, By the next day i got quality alone time with my birth giver. I got my first beaten from Islaine who was determined to show me fear like I was a deer in a mountain lion territory. That was well executed, the first beaten from my birth giver reasoning was me being an eight year old island boy crying he wants to eat still his island Caribbean food and not this American, Western Hemisphere food. Traumatized, I realize my appreciation for my culture and island style dishes following my sacrifice too admit truthfully when I should of lied. Imagine that, I was getting beat while she was driving, this was before " don't text while driving". For my birth giver, the saying would of been " don't hit and drive", funny now but how serious and painful this was that moment is a laughter from me thinking "damn that lady had some hands or hand while the other was still on the wheel" but a head shaker in opposition too her celf hate. A slap to the face, yank of my shirt follow by " shadap, you gonna eat hamburgers, fries". Shut up JaMes I should of told my spirit at the time, but he doesn't, "but I want rice, chicken, peas sauce". Rib cage shot (bam) that hit after that leaves you searching for a lost breathe begging to come back too you at once. Hand to the neck shove follow with wording, "you didn't hear me the first time, shadap". I did , but when you leave, I will talk again, too mycelf, I learned right then to say the least. That was to mycelf. Crying that night, missing Grand Momma in mind thru sights. Scared, am I living with the devil thoughts crossed me from that day on in continuation. My first questioning of my grandmother upraising, "Why would God separate us ?, why would God take good away to deliver me bad", this God hates me". From eight on up to eighteen, I held my feelings secretly about God and religions. Intellectually, I was in no way capable to tell threw those ten years of uncertainty if I was wrong or right about my feelings. I was fueled with do not cross, question, or mock God or else you were the devil child. I never wanted to be the devil child by judgement but ironically this the perfect match too what was offered as my current options growing up at the time. Fear led me to not question, giving in is the alternative. Universally, Religions, believes is bigger than race and cultures. There's more *different races and cultures that shares the same religions then there's religions who shares the same cultures and race. This problem assisted the release of the shackles too religion or believes that I was born in, this problem of swinging on both sides. I prayed yet my spirit question me, "how can you pray to a God none of your image ?", how can you confirm your Christian God is better then any other or religious names of Gods. I simply couldn't. I didn't get this monkey off my back fully but this understanding helped pushed off the monkey that was on the back off the monkey on my back, ya dig !, over stand my comprehension. You don't get a diamond without the return of pressure, everything correlates in this world. I was free to think I was whatever I read or seemed to be yesterday. I was a king until I studied those first biblical or earth Queens and Kings were a little on the tall side, the side race of Nephilim's. Though looked like me in racial content, also did they have slave who was born in melanin skin with wool hair, just as me. My conflict, I'm not capable of ruling out religion, though man made, though man written, still I'm not capable of ruling what I don't know to be exact, if in fact religion is needed for spiritual growth !?. My Ayiti bloodline makes such very hard to do so as my formidable records by his story and artistry which confirms such Atlantic slave trade did occur. This revolutionary fight won in 1804 by my people has an remarkable ancestral artistry that goes all the way back to the Hebrew Israelite story, the twelve tribes of Judah written theory of what was. The Levite tribe is represented as Ayisens in modern content, proclaiming while I disclaim, I see souls more then I see skin, I love my own because we ought to win. Should I hate you or fixate the one who raise you to hate me. My past is not my future. I'm indirect to matters as I perceive every matter differently. Anger, hate, pain is not and shouldn't be normal to hold. I would never accept captivity but did you know running from being captive can actually build you trauma ?. I see atheist, religious, non believers, narcissus, and others who claims a group very happy or maybe it's just an appearance of happiness. No shame, I'll be the first to admit, I'm lost. Comfort zones, although these feel good, this can never fueled me, my mental Diesel engine can not intake regular gas. Intuitively, the world is so big, our universes on earth simply cannot fit our universal minds. The ideas of life I firmly see under celf choices, I humbly say so. Like the boy who tripped me In Ayiti, is all my problems really my mothers fault or me !?, how much is her ?, how much is me?. When I say celf choices, every choice I've done or going to take effects today and tomorrow, past, present, and future. This was the cycle seen through my flesh and spirit warfare that helped me not battle the differences by people anymore as I met the battle of I versus Me. Give in to temptations, be as my mother said, "a bum, thief, prisoner, or a dead man". This made me wonder what must have had been told to her to send that energy towards thy. In most cases, people tend to treat you how there were treated in life or in particular circumstances. Oh how nice is the saying "slap me, I'll give you the other cheek". Heard this but haven't read nor seen this happened visually. Far from perfect, my birth giver scar imperfection on me so I can't feel my worth knowing she was the doer to tell me and show me that exact worth. Imperfection is life, with senses comes perfection. How to get you some sugar canes and purified the juice, squeeze some lemons, apply nature hydration aqua and sip on your masterpiece. As I am, life began showing me who I was. Versatility, my early teenage years battle a wombman looking to keep me down at all causes verses multiple wombman who had a spiritual son who never had a mother was me. One opinions of you is not yours or others opinions of you unless you make such out to be 9........*

Initiative 4:

~ "I'll sleep when I die"

Anxiety was and still too an certain been a life partner of mines mind. Not knowing being alert, focus, restless can be hurtful, I was in my mind more than I needed to be. Incredibly thoughtful, I grew too care despite what wasn't cared for me. Humanly, me inwardly overseeing humanity plagued a care of balancing my worth while uplifting any that I can do the same for as threw humans and nature beings. I am that I am, "AHAYA ASHER AHAYA". For sake, I criticized my kindness with reasonings from my hardship. Too my celf, I can beat up celf inwardly but still be in character of positive outwardly. Not for all or of all but my experience showcased me that majority are simply nosey too others issues of circumstances, not too many ask or care for an intent to help change or assist the matter in a situation. Like Joe, we just wanna know. I always felt my problems wasn't worthy, so I put celf second, third, fourth and so on, but rarely first. Wise years was before I can speak or understand as comprehension been my life calling in seeking gratitude of attitude. I don't regret hate being my first love, my eyes would never have been open to the differences. As my grandmother being my actual first human recalling interactive love, my spiritual, mental, and flesh bond was and forever will be too my birth giver, my goddess as my source by womb, Islaine. What a truth to know and have to live with as the child from which my birth giver is unaware of such power that she contains. Why hate you if I can uplift you !. From leaving Wendy's, to whom someone accuses I of thinking it was my house, lies, that I can't confirm myself, guess I did, grain of salt, I have no proof so much be true is life. Speaking of such, from that day, I knew food wise, the burger was not my thing, I was a plant eating type of kid, some bread and Malta, oooh, you love me if you got me some, preferably Ayisen bread, hot out the oven and the Indian chief Malta, not gonna say the brand, yep, mi book, no clout here to give. Still in love with my yams, plantains, seasoned fish for the Island raise youth. Also I'm into some spicy spices with a nose runner after is my guilty pleasure, or some ginger to rejuvenate my body, bloodstream cleanser. Something about heat makes me get stuck on stupid, "I will finish you, don't test me, I don't care how hot you claim to be, don't play with me". Simplicity, too move on, fries and pizza from the American diet and lifestyle definitely since my arrival have been a bad weakness of choices of taste following the delicacy of snacks and sweets. Dairy and especially cheese I can certainly live without, not lactose intolerant, but likes as oily foods, salty or bitter, my body and taste bud has always been direct with the effect of what I'm putting into my body will be the causes of how I feel later as being energized or sleepy. I like good tastes but I rather greater results over. As my body grew important to me, picky is I, mutuality is my nature. I don't want nothing that don't want me as I don't want such in vice versa. Examples goes from people, places, and things. After leaving Wendy's, at the time did not know any difference in location, my thought process was America is America, 'home of the free". Food is available anytime you want, with lights, clothes, cars, being given as common. As ignorant such may sound, but coming from a third world country, this was heaven on earth at the time seeing options for everything. In the country, options are for the richest too make, choices are for the poor too receive . I knew at eight that people go to work and different jobs pays differently or even the fame and statuses of celebrities that brought higher earning and worshiping by others. Michael Jackson, Jordan, Selena was and still global, as other brands from clothing, sports, musicians, actors, presidents were too. Not that I knew any better from what they did to reach such status, the difference of somebody performing in front of crowds compare to that person as somebody in that crowd is the spectacular and performance aspect I grew up knowing and saw being an chameleon. I'm not much of a watcher, where I'm at, my eyes paint moments by seconds, proactively I create. You don't wanna be in my head, there's no limits in my thoughts of abilities, how can I settle. Nothing was specific. Settling in at what I would know years later as "Deepside", "dem pink apartments cross da library", Lauderhill, FL. Can't remember that first night, I'm not sure if my blood half brotha Bary was there with Gary to pick me up nor remembering encounters with others. Not sure if was at my aunt Tina apartment, my birth giver Auntie, sister of my grandmother, and Mother to my cousin uncle Jean who took me to Port Au Prince, Ayiti. My aunt Tina and I hit it off early as I recalled a trip to which she visited Ayiti and changed her flight or miss her flight due to me crying of her too not leave me and her matching my emotions of not wanting too leave. I won't call her love as sympathetic, now looking back she definitely loved me like she knew what I was going threw and didn't like it nor did she speak out about her views. Auntie Jeannette is my cousins Gary & Greg's mom. Them two pink building in Lauderhill was the "little Haiti" of Broward which made my transition easy from one country too another. In between this "little Haiti" section, from my Great Grandfather "Lépe", my cousin Gary, and my two mother aunties, life was great as long *as I wasn't with my mother. The abuse was not nightly but her and I never loved each other, from what it appears. I will speak for me and not her as this was only my assumptions base of her actions, but certainly for me, I'm scared of you, my first day, you intimidated me to not speak of my desires, I couldn't be a kid and ask this lady for a toy how scared I was of her. Yea right, a toy is not going to be a belt for her to whip my behind with, no thanks, I'll take " keep quite when mothers around" for $5,000 please, final answer. I knew early how I can and not jeopardize my life, so that's one person I couldn't play jeopardy with. So my love I gave back too those who prioritize me with simplicity, love. Hugs, supermarket shopping, caring if I played, eat were the kind of love I grew to go to war for, just a simple care can do magic. Confuses me when people have pure love for me, what do you want ?, a question my mind plays insecurely. My first day in an American school "Royal Palm Elementary" if a word can describe went horrible. I was good until my cousin Gary drop me off in front of my teacher. The truth may sound racist but I was an foreign kid lacking experience in all phases and the truth of my perception is what I have for you. I remember being traumatized by this teacher skin. Purple, greenish veins in her arms, an bob cut blonde hair elderly lady. I look up then look right down several times I recalled, trying to get a picture with my glances without staring. "What kind of human is this?" in my naïve non educated mind at this time I thought. I remember hearing her talking to me, not as me understanding verbally but her body language of bending her back as she waves at me. At this moment*

I'm froze, I don't know where I'm at, I wanna run and find Gary but I have no idea which way he went. Moment then I remember my wrist being grabbed, my heart dropped, fearful in one moment then thought, "please take me to Gary, please take me to my cousin". Wrong, we went into a classroom. Walked me in, I looked up while she still has my wrist with one hand and introduce me with the other hand, pointing to me as the new kid. Another glance I took too see my surrounding, I'd seen other kids. Some melanin, some Caucasian, not sure if I could of tell you any other ethnicities at that time, had no idea of Spanish, Chinese, etc, just as what would be known as "white and black" to me back then. She walked me to a desk and I sat, my backpack unpack, I wasn't going to make one move. I recall an melanin brotha obviously around my age thinking, okay his Ayisen because he was my skin tone, I'm going to ask him for Gary. what I said in creole made his eyebrows raised and then he responded in gibberish too what this sounded like in my ear at the time, the language that I would know to be English weeks after. So after about five minutes, probably under three, don't recall the time specifically but it wasn't long at all, the laughter's and the zoo animal factor of everybody looking or pointing at you with no comprehension made me feel so misplaced. I must of said too mycelf, "yawl gon learn today". I cried non stop from that first school Bell to close the front doors all the way until that two o'clock bell to unlock the front doors. I know I ate tears for lunch but couldn't skip the juice, I needed that apple juice to keep me fluid, we all know how much energy tears and crying can take out of you. That was a day which was 1 of 1, the chameleon in me stayed silent mostly of course, mocking was a trait that came with observing. ABC's, Numbers, Days, Months, taught by my cousin Gary, whose now a certified teacher and football coach, what's meant to be doesn't fall to far from the tree of growth by repetition, an educator from beginning to end. The accent was held for a couple of months but being young and having young ones around me in dem pink buildings helped me to fit in no time with my new American lifestyle. Competition I already developed in Ayiti, athleticism that I was born with allowed me to beat my cousin Gary my second day here in a foot race called by my cousin Greg. Greg got too Gary easily, " you a loser, you loss". His big brother applauding me and laughing at him I presumed hurted but I shown enough was delighted. Competition fueled Gary then and still now, with the bad of his brotha mocking came the goods of his overcoming and fearless mentality. Beat that boy in my "Jesus sandals" at that, "zopop flip flops", leather covered with the strap sandals, Yad Mon Ting. From sports was football and basketball, I played soccer in the streets of Ayiti, though was popular universal, Broward County is football, track and field then basketball, for the urban communities view points, these are the popular sports were so attentive too. Hide and go seek, truth or dare, terrible but "Negro knockin" was our adult ways of clubbing, being adventurous as kids. This game got us too much buttocks whooping when I think about it. Everybody in the buildings knew our parents. "Some bad glutes kids" followed by head shaking was a daily saying too us, not that we did not deserve such reaction. At that we we're *only between nine to ten years old doing these activities. We had an older friend that who was about thirteen years old, three or four years older than me and Gary. He was small from the standpoint of being our size so our age was not of a difference but nowviewing back and thinking, "he was tripping", we weren't his group age. "Negro knockin" which was banging at somebody door and we all run away laughing looking to find a quick hide spot. Making that person open the door looking and asking who is this then going back and forth was so the funniest thing too us at that time, little terrorizers of peace were we. Pissing in the laundry rooms, hallways, going inside evicted apartments to play and be grown was other journeys we've done. This friend who I thought was our age at the time, wasn't doing anything we wasn't doing differently nor pressuring us if not vice versa, me and Gary would be willing and he would say lets not on certain things. Playing grown at our age was ignorant of us in actions but not curiosity. Knowing now he was three too four years older doesn't sit well with knowing we were playing grown with young girls that was our age, Me and Gary. Wrong is wrong so we were wrong together or right living life threw our experiences not by others timing such experiences for us, I know now, playing house is dangerous. "Aww, look at them playing grown, so cute", my private body parts as an young male boy wasn't developed neither was they as young girls, but we acted out our surroundings doings from being. Being young with adult choices simply allows you to grow up faster than you have too. I've been thinking of womban who were then little girls in sexual manners since I was* ten years old, actually younger, definitely played house in Ayiti with one of my girl family members, Live with the truth to grow from. I love you my sista, our love was un normal, should have been crawling but our upraising was too run as soon you can get to, no game plan was given. For us then to be teenagers or growing to our adults not knowing exactly what loosing our virginity meant is my scar of not remembering by actual first inner direct encounter. From playing house, kissing, touching, I did too much extra curricular activities as an child and teenage years that led me too look at sex as just a pleasurable desire run by energy I felt by moments. I've been molested, a close family member of course. Fun fact, in your lifetime you'll be hurt mostly by those closes too you. Don't take it personal, it just a factor of matter of time and what had to be. If you ought to get stuck in an moment, that moment I assure can pull you back whenever such like too, a safe haven to describe you by experience. So important to speak on is molestation just as the childish sexual actions we socially grow to do with no prior education on Sexual Energy Xchange, we must not accept a moment for forever. Sex is just an acronym. Do I hold resentment to whom preyed on me ?, Too a certain extent, it's only natural, for me in honesty, because I wasn't big enough to defend myself, I felt that predator knew that which is the reasoning amongst getting revenge that boils my blood, I know for a fact that predator wouldn't done that too anyone there size, a prey stays away from strength, they search mental, physical, and spiritual weaknesses. I always got that back pain in mind I feel for the young vulnerable me, the adult of me feels that I *owe the child version of me some get backs. The issue I have in keeping hate in my heart or soul you may call such is the celf draining mental hate that you then form forcelf, conveying such time and energy to that person or situation is yours to feel not the other person. Mainly, I take no Losses, I learn time after time. I've always been the same "why me?" Because I cannot control much uncontrollable factors that occurred to me, my weakness is not being able to logically lie too myself in a time that may be deemed negative and telling myself it's positive. The tears and pain from my " why me" hurts because I knew at the end of the day, like the sunsetting after an rainy day, my tears would run dry, feeling that stiffness from what was moist water too my nose flaring to suck up the water from my eyes mix with mucous was those embracing courageous knockdown moments in a boxing match. You down, hearing the ref count "1.2.3", now you on your knees sucking for air. "4.5.6.7.8", before the fingers can flip to shape of the number 9, you up. The ref in your head asks you, " you okay", you nod, "wanna continue fighting", you nod. That's tears of joy. Pretending outward can be your worst enemy living inwardly. If you notice, there's no comfort spot anywhere for a broken heart too lay peacefully. Indecisiveness will keep you up as there's no placement you can lead on to rest assure by comforts need. We delay our inner truths constantly for the outer appearance that can break your reasoning to ever speak. empowerment is your guide, intuitively, we all know what to do or what's needed to be done. The cycle always seems to be easier being apart of then against. Raped Fathers & Mothers physically, spiritually and mentally have no morals or principles, this just the way of victims. Hurt people hurt people. Lack of education on the body, genders , and stages of development is the freedom gateway for Molestation, teen pregnancy, mental confusions of sexual desires or partners. If the hurt person never admit, there mostly gonna react as the abuser, that feeling of doing what was done too you is human nature. You don't learn by staying in your bubble that you think is all in totality. All is capable to learn from only if one pass away, then I cannot tell you what happens there after. There's more silent hurt people then there's vocal courageous people. If you were taught to be silent in the face of nature, then you were taught to treat darkness as light........9*

Initiative 5:

~ Power feels like You

Overcoming always been the obstacle, how can I rest when I'm so far behind !?, how can I sleep with all on my mind. Fourth grade, a new beginning was in front of me once again. My birth Giver Islaine was moving, "7520 nw 23rd street, Sunset Strip, FL". Can't recall whom move first between us all, Auntie Jeannette, Auntie Tina all I recalled ended up moving from "dem pink apartments" to different locations, same city of course but for kids who were living in the same building, that was the equivalent move to NY from FL at the time. This is when I met what would become my step father Levelt, day one cool guy, respected me and some way confused me by this respect. I mean the culture of the Ayisen lifestyle is built so much on "respekte granmoun", respect your elders. I don't disagree in the wise sense but it's an one sided sword that cuts multiple ways. Your taught to obey, don't disobey, again nothings wrong with that besides masters laid down the same laws for there slaves. Most island parenting see's the combination of protection and control as a positive way to express there love and possessive and abuse being positive disciplinary actions. As you can view, All parents are great parents in the Island mindset if food, clothing, and shelter is provided. Control is not an option too have as an celf thinker, but being an possession is an direct link to a slave master, an island parent see's protection as the aide to cure danger. Though protection has its perks, the flaws too such normally keeps that child inexperienced and dishonest base on true desires for living. The vibe from Levelt helped me give people chances that I thought I could or never would before. He cared to build a relationship with me separately then the fact that you're just a kid I have to deal wit. You deal with me, I don't have to deal with you is most men ideology as an stepfather . I'm now a one Saturday morning, Pokémon, wrestling American kid, at least I perceived to be. The experiences Television showed life can be and offer, this made me gullible, I wasn't any different, I can be normal and have anything another kid had was the exploitation my heart felt from the country foreigner to the American boy. Attending a school closer to my new area of living, I went to "Village elementary fourth to fifth. September 26th was originally September 9th in my head. Never having an birthday celebration, none in Ayiti and in America. My excitement grew from what could be, I've seen kids come to school on there birthday where there guardians brings sometimes, games, music, snacks and of course cake or cupcakes, 'Yum yum yum" goes the classrooms on birthdays in Elementary . My teacher asked us all, not sure if on the first day of school or the second week when was our birthday. Confidently I said September 9th with no hesitation. At this time in my life, I know the important of months and what day of the week is and was it. The dates in months had no significant meaning for me, Monday-Friday, Friday night meant I'm having an one on one candle light dinner with the Disney channel, Nickelodeon. No school Saturday, one Saturday morning and heading to my aunties Jeanette or Tina was the safe havens, Sunday sad but excited for the weekend to be over with but the school friends and playtime was not to shabby, Elementary was not hard. Teacher then said "ok great, I'll get you some cupcakes and snacks on the 9th of September". Not sure if I asked my birth giver the year prior or because the teacher asked but when I asked " when's my birthday", her response was "September". "Okay thank you', I automatically assumed it was the ninth day and didn't even bother to ask her more details like the time, was I crying, how long was labor ?. Writing now, I know it was fear and being uncomfortable, I couldn't be around my birth giver without anxiety kicking my guts, expect the unexpected was what I knew when around Islaine . Looking at an calendar, counting and seeing September as the ninth month, like a fool in mind, my birthday was September 9th. I remember seeing those little numbers boxed in together from 1-31 thinking 'those too much numbers, can't be birthdays". Somethings made me uncertain when other kids confirm theirs, " my Birthday is September 15", "I'm December 21" another goes. Okay those numbers clearly meant something I thought now but the 9th I already claimed, was not switching in my mind. September 9th came, I'm excited, put on the best outfit I had. You wouldn't know nothing about those "silk dragon ball Z" shirts with some "And1 slip ons" shoes, thought I was the man, I cant deny. I was happy, told my birth giver it's my birthday today, she laugh hysterically, she was slapped mentally by me, of course something she never knew physically. Not gonna ruin my day I thought, I got a party to go too, my party. As

49

stated she would, my teacher got the snacks and cupcakes. I don't wanna make any name up but can't recall her name, You are appreciated Miss spirit teacher lady. As all birthdays, we would put the games, snacks everything away and the party started during lunch time. Lunch comes around, I'm excited, not just for the birthday party we're gonna have but I've been waiting anxiously for the "beep beep beep beep, Happy Birthday" moment. Got lunch, put my lunch number in and no response. My teacher looked down and asked, "you sure it's your birthday?". I know now for sure it was not after not getting a notification from the keypad, I lied still and yes to save the embarrassment. I thought I got away with a lie but looking back, she must of agreed to actually save me the embarrassment. The snacks and cupcakes where eaten of course, then out we went to P.E. physical education. Coming back from P.E., my teacher pulled me to the side and said, "I went to the office and check your profile", " your birthday is September 26, see". Showing me on the paper, I said, "okay" looking straight down at my feet after. Embarrass gain, again because I felt bad earlier for not really knowing but still telling her yes, I remember her looks of concern, at that I thought was her being mad that I lied and would say something like "I'm going to tell the principle and class you lied to me about your birthday", but she didn't, held my hand "lets go back to class" she stated. Years later, I realized this was a shocking sympathetic moment of 'wow, you did not know your birthday'. Days later gone by, truly I wasn't counting, thought I never had before, why be sad about now. Unexpectedly, a regular day in my head where I go

*to apply my lunch number the boom, "Happy Birthday".
That robot voice machine have no idea how much I felt
alive in that moment which was on September 26. I'm
assure now I got the date correct, I was able to confirm
and got all my paper work when I was 14, looking to get
my first W-2 job . Once I got away from school that day
September 9th, I remember walking home piss, "how
come I didn't know my own birthday". Usually in fear of
my mother, not saying hello but just what was direct in
my mind, only one question I needed an answer for ," is
September 26 my birthday !?", she responded with a
mellow voice, "Yes". She must of felt my energy, one
moment I can actually say my birth giver actually
sympathize with how I felt. Though she gave no extra
response or time too, I knew she dropped the ball, and
she knew she fumbled what she carried, which was her
own creation. Celf guilt doesn't need to be said or
shown, intuitively, you can always, I guarantee, FEEL
9........*

Initiative 6:

~ The Young Old Man

I grew up living supporting the future while looking at me as the past, I was my bare truth I couldn't mask. My cousins Steve and Valentina where my first two young siblings and kids mentally. On the aspect of being knowledgeable too my life, doing great for them did me great inwardly, so important is this for me to let the future know there worth in the presence before the presence gave them an idea of there worth by past experience. I spent my middle school years at "Bair middle School" in sunrise FL, the beginning of being an adolescent adult. We left Elementary, not separated by much, maybe clothing choices and curfew time differences, so much was on the way as change was to continue as different days . Middle school is the epitome of an young life crisis. Sexual hormones development, "you got cooties" turns to a note " I like you, do you like me back, check yes or no", "can I walk you home ". Money I would say was the biggest change in my life at this time, we're all as kids felt the effect as our feet's got bigger, the shoe prices were not the same for our family. The hairstyles for young girls cost more, we needed and wanted more, experiences were to bought from adventures, Imaginations were for kids of all sudden, we wanted to see or do now. Sixth grade was almost like my first day at Royal Palm Elementary, Horribly bad. Not the in language barrier difficulty or not having friends but more so grade wise, I simply went bad, all Fs the first semester followed by C's and D's second semester took me to summer school that led me to Seventh Grade. Candy man was me seventh and Eight grade as I had a plug. A connect, someone who assisted me by fronting me the product, then I go to sell however much and return an percentage from the front load which was given. Frantzdy was my connect, one my brother Bary partners. Respect too my elders like ralph and Tangy, friends of my brotha, street wisdom can't be bought or price tagged . My brother Bary always been soft to me, maybe I just saw him as an loud attentive momma boy. Too a degree, my perception was right and wrong. My sister Vanessa was the youngest out of my birth giver Islaine womb. Being the middle child taught me some ways of positive and negative. I was able to see in my teenage years that my mother was not choosing to hurt me personally but all who she created. My perspective of viewing my sister, my birth giver only daughter and her last birth creation. An wombman she's now just as my birth giver, too have not feelings or any connective upraising to her mother hurt me still now and as a young man prior, Ayiti had showed me that boys are to leave there village and start a life while the young girl is groomed to be a wife. As a young man in America, though I was not in the streets in the form of gang violence, narcotic selling, or even a partying type, my birth giver knew my future was either in the streets, locked up, or dead, never gave her a reason to proclaim such, she just thought it would be great for me to know so I can act out her perception. Harsh words that I never felt a bond to do by actions. For a mother to have a daughter and at four months old, packed her up to her dad and never look back. This mother was the same birth giver who I came out of and sent away after six months and first born child father was absent just like all the others. The difference from my understanding between my sister and I compare to my brotha was that he was her first child. I cannot say precisely her attachment reasoning to not abandon my brotha as my sister and I were. Could it be an her attachment towards him being the first?, could it be that it's easier to move on with guys and state the case to say I have only one, not two nor three kids ?. Though my brotha was there, I cannot say he's upraising was any better then mines, nor can't confirm precise occurrence in his livelihood. I do know he lived with her though he was constantly being watch by someone else and had no connection to his father. The mental, spiritual, physical abuse, the different men he would have to encounter continuously, are facts of his life and upraising I saw occurred in vice versa too me. Hurt people hurt people, I don't condone any pain. You realize so much the cycle of evil, a cycle of get back, you smack my left I smack your right, an eye for an eye. The attention my brotha graved so much from Islaine is for which the reason I called him soft earlier. In opposite, he received the same "you gonna be in the streets, locked up, or dead" treatment, the difference, he believed and accepted coming from his Goddess creator. The power of an wombman is underestimated, every real man yearns understanding with his wombman, yearns her admiration. Mothers,

Sisters, aunties, Wife, Wombman, "Happy life - Happy Wife". No real man want to feel worthless around any wombman, now imagine that when the wombman you love don't love you back, a deranged man is what you get. Stealing was our go to and I must admit between my fifth grade and threw my seventh grade year, though we wasn't tight, the common factor for both of us was no assistance. No robbing hoods, I was just out for robbing goods. I fell back from the corner stores, pharmacy, retails and grocery robberies as my psych developed to understand cause and effect, karma, What goes around comes back around. As I fell the streets ranking, I wanted that Disney American kid life with the picket fence home, my brotha graduated to more streets activities and violence. Gangs, drugs, streets codes, which there our non but everyone in the streets vows to live under. The point of this factor is me being wise beyond my years, I promise too you, I felt my brotha sacrificed for me base upon his actions. It was the perfection of "look little bro, everything I'm about to do in high school and moving forward, you ain't suppose to do". Though he never said this to me, this was exactly how I perceived it, just as he's "do not" show me what not to do, same in vice versa was the opposition of what I can do. We don't speak, honestly I speak to none of my blood siblings, not the intention but the upraising have us separated by time spent together. From our birth giver to us all as siblings, never been a line in communication that was consistent. I was average threw out middle school in all phases. Too cool do the work but too smart to not pass the class. Perhaps I could have been Mister Popular but my insecurity from my smile was not something I adorn, so my personality of creativity and inner happiness athletically wasn't shared easier outwardly unless comfortable with you. How you gonna crack on me about having a missing tooth when I just simply wouldn't smile or talk with my bottom lip so you wouldn't see !?, "want be the butt of your jokes" was my insecure strength of thought. This covering up would hurt then and moving forward. When asked for assistance on the things I needed, Islaine simply laughed or ignored. By example, I know this sounds harsh but it was almost like asking the devil or an negative entity to be nice. Imagine that, "Umm, hey, my life you making a little too hard, you mind taking it easy on me for a while?". What kind of answer you expect from such entity?, good luck with an good one........9

Initiate 7:

~ Daring trutha

Jealousy from my brotha and mother was so normal, I thought they was plotting on me. Put your view to that, every time you had love ones come over, your heart felt light & free and soon as there gone, your worried you're gonna be attacked not knowing which one will be doing so. I'm an lover of growth so maturity loves me back. A hater seeing this became a sight too destroy me any ways possible. Levelt being a blessing that he already was, blessed me even more with a brotha Steve "Bobby" "Smoke" Corneille. Cousins Evans, "E-Money" and Rolin, "Sasha" that even out my household balnce. I had my haters and those I know wanted me to progress. "What do you say you like most in a girl JaMes ?", "umm, how she look !?", "No, her personality" Evans responded. The Montreal, New York drip mix with the southern Hood was my versatile household that gravitated my clothing, music, girls, and the way I made my moves by choices. My brotha Smoke made me cried a couple times, never from hardship of his doing to me but being one of the first too see my struggles and being hurt by the doings too me. "Why she doing you like that !?", "that's not right !", "but you ain't do nothing !?". These words of truth always brought tears because there my thoughts inwardly but I always hid because simply I didn't know anyone else saw my situation as I interpreted. A million and one. A million can treat you wrong but one can save you strong, Thankful. Summers were my heaven time. Between all my middle school years, my Summers were split either at my aunts Tina or Jeannette's home, where I was actually an priority for those living in. I was going to seventh and my cousin Gary was going to eight. I remember him coming too my house on sunset strip with two boys who I would be friends with in continuation by life's giving. He, "Jon", and "Dexx" road there bikes too my house as Gary advise the boys he knew where they can get some condoms. Better be save then sorry right ?. If you had it, looks like you were going too use or had use such before. I believe it was my birth giver friend of hers who brought a big pack from the clinic joking too Islaine base on all the boys that was in one house, If she didn't want to babysit as a young grandmother then she would be wise to make sure we use condoms for protection. I was the youngest with my brothas Smoke & Bary, and cousins Evans & Rollins. Apparently, lifestyles pop too easy and rough riders were uncomfortable for the my older peers in the house, so at twelve, I had a bag of protection with no action so all I can do is brag about this, showing my pack off at school was like having bullets too a gun. From my peers at school to my cousin Gary, having condoms instantly made me 'the man", It was like having, grown men money type of respect. Them boys road there bike to me from 44th and university down to sunset strip too get some condoms. "Sup, Yawl boys need some condoms" I asked, "Yea just one a piece each would be cool". My cousin Gary is a year older than me and at the time I thought them boys was really going to utilize so I responded, "yawl boys straight, take the bag". My homies been my homies since. We then got greedy and went to still some magnums from a store weeks later, mission successful but karma got our bikes stolen while we were in the store stealing, Life, Lessons. These summers changed me from the childhood friends that became, the families of friends, my friends which became family. I'm not sure how Jon & I got so tight immediately, I really can't recall, from the perspective of him and Gary were school friends prior and I met him threw Gary. From that day of coming to get protection from me, we always stayed connected. Jon & Brandon are brothers, Zach & Jordan are brothers. Caleen, my first mother by actions are Jon & Brandon moms who sister, Auntie Jacqueline is Zach and Jordan's mom. Francis, "Pops" and Barbara Jim are the parents to Caleen, Jacqueline, and Auntie Sandra. From Jamaica, not sure if both were born and raised in Montego Bay but eventually departed for more opportunity in the U.S as most from the islanders does. Settling in New York and raising there three daughters, The Jim's family got bigger as the girls became adults, growing as wombman and bringing life into this realm. If you wondering what this have to do with my life ?, why is all this important in my book ?. I ponder and think what if Francis and Barbara never met ?, what if I never was able to get my info back from when someone else was living under my name in America. Back to the religious or believes standpoints earlier. I'm firm on the idea that nothing happens from a chance, accidentally, or mistakenly reasoning. Is there a creator to life, someone or something having the divine intellect of the birth and death of life. 50/50 is being uncertain but I'm one hundred percent sure I do not know. I cannot deteriorate my life and say I was the controller to the effects by my causes nor can I say someone or something else did. I do know, help or assistance from others is something I feel spiritually was the creator or biblically speaking, a religiously way I've gotten assisted by. My reasoning by examples is those aunties, step brothas, my Jamaican family, those who seen good in me without me seeing such within mycelf. That's powerful, those are things I had no idea would be provided to me but was. This are things and people I always needed but didn't know I would receive. Jon as my brotha was just like my brotha Steve from the idea he wasn't blind, he saw my hands under the table before I would manipulated the cards I was dealt. He carried a heavy heart from me since, that gets to me at times because I felt I was the brotha who held us back in our friendship, the one who took away from us just being kids. Instead of bringing me five, we're sharing your five, an humbled burden was the feeling for me growing up. "Im not hungry" as my stomach growls was the type of kid I was that grew to the men I am. Close mouth don't get fed so a lot of malnutrition days for JaMes. The summer of going to ninth grade, I chose to go too Piper High school for two reasonings. Going to plantation High School, I knew I was gonna get into the street activities as most of my friends from Bair middle and those who stayed off sunset strip would be attending. Scared ?, not quite !, again learned from my brotha and surroundings of course, why do what I knew already or seen the results from. Now being a teenager, going to a more mixed school, playing sports, and being around my summer true friends instead of hanging out only during the summer was my reasoning. Anytime I can get away from my birth giver was a great time. Worst factor was now, I was the only kid left in the house as Bary joined the streets full time, Smoke going to college for football, and my cousins Evans and Rolin leaving the house *brought a one sided perspective that I knew already too well from experiences. Most get cut off or doing for between eighteen and twenty one, I am one of one, I was pushed off the porch earlier. I recall the summer heading to high school, as I was Packing and getting ready to leave for my aunt Jeannette's home, Islaine goes " just know I'm not buying you nothing, you going to High School, good luck", certainly my quote is not precise, one her saying this in creole and the words weren't too nice, I can assure that. Whatever I thought, " Bye lady", I was the type where I'm not taking a day off that I can have away from my birth giver, I'm going to need every second that I can use to get away. The week before summer starts, I'm calling my aunties letting them know I'm ready to leave, come and get me, ASAP. Summer was fun but I also knew now I wasn't getting nothing to start the school year with. Having a year advantage over me, Gary and Jon was heading into there sophomore year and wanted better clothes and money to do more in there high school journey. That was perfect, I was swimming and my brothas came aside on a boat and said we're heading to your destination, hop on. On the bikes that summer, we looked for jobs during the days, played during the nights. We all got hired at Wendy's but Jon and Gary ended up getting another opportunity at an restaurant name "Cheddars" at the time. Perfect I'm thinking, perfect. Now I have to come back for uniform and paperwork to get started. I needed an ID. My school ID was not valid and needed a state ID as an requirement. Ok I thought, just need to get my social card and birth certificate from Islaine to get this completed. I* remember taking the bus back to Islaine home the same day in the summer so I can get this completed. I was proud and confident, "I don't need your help anyways, I'm a man, I'll work for it", thoughts walking from the bus stop to my birth giver home. I remember her quilting something while watching TV and I was like "I got a job", silencefilled the room. In my head, " such a hater", moving on, " I don't have a state ID so I need my birth certificate and social so I can go make one". No hesitation for her quick response this time, " I'm not helping you nothing", now I'm silent but thinking, "I got a job, what did I do wrong here". I went into the garage which was the boys room, my room, like an actual garage door, knock and I'll look between the garage door handlers. I was waiting until my savior at the time Levelt too arrive home. I was mad more than I can care about her reasoning. I did a good deed I thought. I did what I normally never do, I went to ask for help. "Daddy, I got a job and need a state ID, I ask her but she don't wanna help me?". I remember him being happy and was like "no problem, I'll get the paperwork for you, Good job Jimmy, proud of you". Not too long after, a one sided argument erupted with "I'm not helping him, he's too disrespectful " she muttered, follow by him with " Cheri, Cheri, Cheri", "he got a job, what's the problem". He's disrespectful was her only go to and couldn't explain a specific time or what made to be as she explained. Ouch went my heart, determined was my soul. On the bus I went back to my aunt, I knew she wasn't gonna help and close mouth don't get fed. My aunts Tina and Jeannette would ride for me. Tina not in this situation, she felt there's no reasoning my birth *giver wouldn't wanna help me, I must of disrespected truly for her not to help me get this job she thought. My aunt Jeannette was shocked, "what are you telling me your mom not helping you ?, let's go". Vroom we go leaving Aunt Jeannette's too Islaine off Sunrise. I was confident because that "he's too disrespectful" line would certainly need an direct reasoning or example behind her wordplay. "Islaine, James got a job and what is this I'm hearing you don't wanna help him get an ID he needs for work !?". "I refuse to help him, he's too disrespectful". My eyes rolled but this time she had her reasoning too I was disrespectful. I cried after but reminiscing now, it made no sense which too why my aunt Jeannette understood such and didn't even call me out but simply listen to what she was saying. Though today, my inner strength prevails me to think I should have been strong enough to hold my emotions but there's no way I could of have. I'm receiving a murder charge but was never acquitted nor did I go to trial, at that moment I was being sentenced with no appeal. "Jeannette, the other day my son is at the bus stop, I see him, "James, James, James" I call him. Jeannette there's over twenty people at the bus stop with him, he screams " blank you, you stupid blank, leave me alone". I say please my son, please let me take you home, do you know he walks in front of my car, window down and spit on my face, then spit again saying "blank you", you think I'm gonna help him, no way, he's too disrespectful". From the beginning of her reasoning, I remember not even blinking once, no drops but waterfalls. Regardless how stupid or untrue was that story, the pain I felt I still feel, for the womb that I came* out of too degrade me and depreciate herself left me at a lost, confused. Mothers who kids that received "C's" in school would turn that story by stating there child actually got a "B" too families and friends. My "C's" where talks of "F"s" and being disrespectful. As these tears failed, shockingly I remember just looking at her shaking my head but became stronger from that lie . My tears drew to my aunt Jeannette looking at me crying only response after hearing her story was " Oh yea !" as she would look at me and down to her feet, wanting to say more but felt it wouldn't be wise if she did so. Wiping my tears, my aunt Jeannette said " well, I came to try, you said no, I'll bring him back the week before school, let's go JaMes". As low as I felt being that my birth giver lied on me, not even thirty second out the drive way, My Aunt says "I know she lying, you didn't do that", this brought more tears instantly, this today I would know to be then were tears of joy, relieved. This proceeded us to take over six different trips to the social security office, plantation hospital, department of children and families and so on. My auntie was getting a lot of hard times from some people I recalled due to her not being my legal guardian. To that extent, determined and willing, it was someone who felt my pain by my aunties passionate pursuit. Her desire and willingness to help provided us with a copy my social and birth certificate. Where there's a will, there's a way 9……..

Initiative 8

~ Infinite Love

Sex as I explained earlier was educated by experience not my surrounding. Meaning what I knew I did, what did not know I learned. Before I was a man, I had a plan. I was a baby thinking babies. Very young, I had dreams of being my father as husband and my mother being my girl by wife. That's correct, fatherless and motherless kids turns to adults who needs there partner to be something in which they never had, this In which what I would call a punctured heart or love on dialysis. My first love was just as explained. I was her dad boyfriend as she was my mom girlfriend, complications when kids pretend. So early do we yearn unity and some of the strongest unity's comes so early because of the rebel innocence of lacking experience. Young love will have you war ready, put it all on the line because your experience threw mental capacity is limited yet so focus too what is known. No love can be as your first as compare to others, you realize so much you've done.

From every experience there on after the first becomes checks or X marks, what is good or not good for you. The worst factor in most young love is actually not being ready, not knowing celf yet eager to live and do as please. Love is sold, sex is trained in our mental psyche socially. Spiritually we know limited information to what our body does pertaining in moments of fluid exchange. We're taught the outcomes of either pleasure, pregnancy or diseases but not the mental or spiritual effects. The energy xchange is an sacred realm that allows anyone near your soul by the body exchanging fluids, this become the first give away of soul attachments. The man in our society fulfillment is based on numbers. "One time is fine with me if that number allows me to be free to get too another two or three".

Worst is wombman, marriage has been on her mind before her body development is prioritize, too give love is how we learn, giving love to celf, we never learn or educated about this need or how important this shall be. Experience by multiple is her worst nightmare, she's deemed classless, lacking control, a female dog if not performing her training as an demented old circus monkey. Performing the same trick, she's to hide her true talents or any other tricked learned threw her journey. As the man is rewarded by mistake, the wombman gets no room for, a mistake becomes her title by definition. By physic, civilization made this out to be an egoistical chest match between genders, leaving wombman to play checkers while man play chess. Being chosen or be lucked out has an ignorance of displeasure. For this to be a mans world would mean he comes into this world own his own, yet it is from the wombman universe that births his own inner world. The power of a men strength is overlook by the power of whom carried such man. A myth, the lies denounce the notion of life principle of gender. Energy, feminine and masculine is not about the sex of an male or female but mirroring the mental and spiritual energy. If masculine meant man then anger would only be relinquished to the man gender specie as vice versa sensitivity would meant for only wombman. Simply not true, duality showcase we're different by organs but not by mindset. Even the body as masculinity appears majority of the time to be bigger then feminisms physically, this however is not an direct truth beside of that being an opinionated truth as heights, weights and body type is not specific too one gender. I love too hard, I expect perfection from me. I love too strong, I protect love enough where love wants too ponder on other avenues of what can be. You got my trust, I'll be your walking angel. One time is always enough, your break such trust, forgive yourself, it's freezing in hell if you're waiting for my forgiveness. I forgive just can't forget. I'm very disinterested in altercations, some where upraise to be expressive, some raised to shut down and keep to celf. Celf raised mostly, I was raised by raising celf to defend, protect and provide understanding. I defend when being belittle or attacked for my views. I protect when my spirit is being challenged to alter my ways for the better ness of someone else do's. Understanding is my gateway, the aid to provide such in any giving moment. These factors I know I am by experience, all not great all not bad. Anytime I've been done wrong, the answer of why is from within. Anytime I've done wrong, the answer was me. Inside I said lives a universe, how I can I blame this little earth for my universal problems. Wanted to be but never was man enough, my relationships with most wombman were simple if were not together. I don't lie about my needs or desires, in fact at times, I'm simply too honest, words I've heard from those who wanted a lie from a fantasy perspective. Together was the complications for me as I am an natural provider, builder. Lacking stability and structure is not something you don't never want to be in search for before building anything from an relationship, materialistic or spiritual standpoint. With no foundation, you'll spend your life free styling too whatever is in front of you, mimicking your surrounding of is this what I'm suppose to do. Way too good at goodbyes and a tad bit friendly for an hello. The curse of my past is letting go easily and the length of time I spend holding on. Understanding such, I hold the respect of my choice and let go love that I can't attached. In my relationships, my anger dismisses my partners wrong doings, Logical too how I feel but I'm always wrong to not act, instead of acting, I give out what I understand, in such understanding are the words that separate rather then integrate me and my partner. I always had the problem of letting a wombman get the best of me, I've never said it but ultimately this was my way of not allowing you to be my birth giver, to allow you to dictate my views was too not love my celf I feel. In retrospect, experience shown me, everybody does not walk such how they talk such. Logically i crew to think, reacting after a cause came into effect. Both of the wombman I loved at one point in my life, followed by the fact we tried creating life together, did not work.

Now they both have new borns. My heart becomes purer once I let go of someone or something that was known as love prior. Loving that something or someone is so easy when not attached, I'm now able to love that something or someone with no fear of losing or controlling this love, I simply want this love too maturate. My dependency on doing for that someone or something brings a stress, anxiety free zone that is uplifted once out the situation. At peace I can love again for the reasoning that I loved, not for the reasoning of keeping such love. It is written, "MAKTUB"........9

Initiative 9:

~ The Transition

As the Butlers, Scarlett's, Jim's family became the experience of differences for me, the burden of being fatherless and motherless kept me limited to the love giving out to me or too accept purely as genuine. From my early teenage years too my mid twenties, The dinners, trips, games, vacations, I was living moments I never dreamed off or could be possible for me. What some are born with, same are those left to accept as normal, expected of things been completed without no actions from celf. Reincarnated by others doing, I could not be around this family and not learn brotha hood from my brotha's Jordan, Zach, Brandon, and Jon. Sista hood from my the mothers Caleen and Jackie, Mother and father hood from the grandparents Francis and Barbara. So strong did I see these two wombman as Goddesses, prevailing in differences as one Caleen became a mother figure too me as everyone around us seen how close Jon and I became, being my brotha, it was only fitting of her being my mother. Auntie Jacqueline wisdom and spirit grasp me early, "so cool", her vibes and treatment of others, you'll be motivated before receiving hate from, you'll be assisted before being abandoned. You did not have to do for me exactly, I just needed to see what was in your heart by actions too accept your love and be okay in your surroundings. In my younger days, I resented my friendship with Jon with the idea that you sympathizing me, you don't see me as equal, my his story saddens you, you just feel bad, insecurely, my way I grew looking at assistance, always questioning. Always felt I've a been a broak Ritch men, my spelling is correct, broke and oak unified. My pride kept me to say, never look down on yourself or place something or someone else on an pedestal, this became my spiritual intuitive ways. Confident in making something out my celf, my eyes were my first paint brush that can make a dirt empty road appearing with fascinated lighting on and off the road and sightseeing that would make you park just to spectate. The writer I am today always been intaking, I take in more then I could give out, so the pressures been heavy. At the age of 16, I thought I knew everything, I couldn't separate my celf from what a grown man is and was. My sophomore year started off with where I left off my freshman year. Unstable and unprecedented too my actions. No grades forced me to not play football my sophomore year. At this time, I became complacent, the home of my aunties were my refuge from a lonely world. From Jeannette, Tina, and Jacqueline mix with Ol Girl Caleen's home, I abused from the perspective of getting older physically but younger by just wanting to be a kid by these foundations I have now but not when I was younger. I was stuck to be honest on missing a childhood not realizing this already surpassed me and now I'm closer to being a full adult as bills and dependency became the normal life for me. Most kids with bad grades are not bad nor stupid but in school every kid knows, being bad means your just cool, a rebel too what everybody else is doing in a assembly line. Sleeping in school, not caring about my grades, keeping to myself was my cool bad ways. I was lost, I did not see school as an opportunity but just a control factor for most kids to do as said say or what was said to be successful. I always felt school wasn't for me mostly because my lack of support of no system. Being homeless, sleeping in parks, friends home, what and how I was gonna eat today did not match an average high school kid life by mindset in care about, so I was an natural rebel. By the second month of my sophomore year, I recalled being in class, the intercom system on blasting, "can you send JaMes Bastien to principal office, JaMes Bastien". I can't recall my teachers name but remember acting cool as all the other kids went, "ooo, what you did ?", "I don't know, too many to think about" was my response. Leaving the portable my heart panic like, " what I do ?", the principal office call meant you stepped over the administration office most definitely concluded to being suspended or expelled I thought. I get to the office, I remember the principal a bald head melanin guy, "JaMes, sorry you have too leave us but your mother came to withdraw you men", "Huh", looked to my left as Islaine was there looking away. The principal then said "you can finish the rest of day, just sign the withdraw papers". He was sort of confused to why I was hurt not wanting to leave piper but Islaine was adamant that I must go to Plantation. This was on an Friday, he lastly said to return all books by next week Friday or else this would be owed and be kept on bookings I must pay in order to graduate. I was living with my aunt Tina, who lived maybe five minutes away from Piper. What occurred was I we're suppose too be going back and forth from Islaine after school and on the weekends, just using my aunt's address for school territory purposes. After a couple weeks into my freshman year, I moved fully to my aunties, not seeing any reasoning to go back to Islaine and waste my weekends as an servant. My school is right here so why be late every morning taking the bus or walking from sunset strip, my close brotha's and friends lived on this side, why am I going back on the weekends ?, no sense I thought of this nonsense. Islaine got her get back on me as my legal guardian, I had no choice. The rest of the day was not cool, as I'm there reminiscing in the moment that I'll be leaving angered and saddened me. Shake my head was the feeling disappointed and frustrated, after school we did the normal, went to Jon's, ate some food, watch tv then outside to play catch. I remember it was dark but no later then eight as I made my way back to my aunt Tina. My grandmother Louisa was living with Tina at the time followed by another nine to ten family members, yes this was normal in most West Indies household too which I've experience. She never really stayed as my Grandma heart desired understanding from her language and food Ayiti provided. Her body and mind getting older, the best opportunity was in the U.S., though she always felt as a second class citizen in regards to being left at home while everybody at work and watch a tv, my Grandma lack of comfortability made me comprehend her indecisiveness to rather be home then to live alone, mentally. I was young and some what naïve, again I trusted mostly everybody in that house but I realize the trust for me was not the same when it came too we. I was fooled once thinking shame on my birth giver, I was a fool twice to think I can express my truth to the mind she's already manipulated. Everybody's on the couch I remember walking in. Some disappointing faces, some angry faces while I'm walking, mentally in mind " I don't know what happened to you all but my day was not the best neither". "Auntie, can you believe Islaine came to withdraw me from Piper today ?", no response from her as she kept her sight and looks straight. I'm puzzled on the scene and reaction by facial expressions let me knew something had happened that referred me getting this

cold treatment I was receiving now. "That's a shame
how you disrespected your mother at school today, you
deserve that !" Uncle Johnny riddled. I'm thinking,
"what!?", not even what you talking about but "huh!?".
" Yes JaMes, why would you that too your mom" uncle
Jean outburst. This feeling of confused was not quite
new, almost match the feeling of "I got a job since you
said your not gonna help me, I just need my paperwork
to get an ID", just for that same person to say no I'm not
helping you get an ID confusing feeling moment drew all
back to me again. The story Islaine provided her family
while I was still in school to control the narrative was
that she went to Piper to bring me lunch, what a
thoughtful mother anyone would think. The principal
then call me to the office too which when I admittedly
saw her I went on a rampage with curse words and
enough threats to where the principal is holding me
back because I'm looking to fight her. Her story
continues to say, shocked, the principal shouts at me
"this is your mother, she loves you, she brought you
food", too which I responded "who cares, she can die
right now". Embarrass she stated she was, she then
advise the principal, "it's okay, let him go back to class".
I made such a scene the whole administrative office
came to see what the ruckus was about and saw her
crying from such pain. From the principal and other staff
members telling her she doesn't deserve such treatment
for me eventually gave her the reasoning to take me out
of Piper. In my lifetime, from my birth givers closes
friends and family, there's always been a couple saying
about her back to me. " You know how she is", "don't
pay attention to her, she's always angry", " Me and her

*not talking base on what she said to others about me",
"it's her way or the highway". As imperfect she my birth
is and was, I can respect her direct response to people,
she's an liar at heart to never admit any wrongfulness,
however she'll defend her soul and viewpoints as if she's
alone and know one has ever done the same for her, too
which her and I share such pain I can admit this
mutuality upraising experience. In this upraising, Smiling
in your face while there eyes rolled back in disgust was
the way of life. Nosey people need senses by stories to
enhance there smell, most time you get attention just
for that person to get information from you, it's the way
of the universe, we all wanna know what we don't
know. Too a friendly human, "what happened" is an
gateway to express but can't never decode the
reasoning of such question. Where you win, you can
loose. Where's there's pain, you can gain. Where's there
help, there's captivity. Celf observant, Celf Awareness,
Ownership, Risk, experiencing are all cycles that every
soul must go threw at a point of time. Love you, don't
run away from, run too Love you 9……..*

Conclusion:

~ There's none !

My actions, diet, languages, experiences, relationships are still processes of growth that I have not fully obtain. Infinite are my abilities, limited by the shackles in my mind. Lets speak soulfully. If spirituality is the continuation of one spirit experiences and understanding from one flesh too another, then I've been living for an eternity, from the beginning. Wisdom of information at times I never knew of until my eyes are drawn too, my body is felt threw, my noses then senses, my ears is heard true. The same voice from the beginning, "your crazy if you talk to yourself !?". No, this is simply an intuitive conversation. "Your wrong if you define meanings from your viewpoint !", No, the truth is in the eye of the beholder. So important to me is for me to express what saved celf, my spirit. I live by my code of ethics, "do on to others as you would like to be done too you", "the flesh is in an constant search for instant gratification, find your soul before your body". As I livid duality, my peace comes from my abilities, my frustrations comes my experiences. Think about versatility being in a box, just does not fit. Wanting, needing and craving more of what I can is my ultimate sacrifices. Today I am the youngest I've ever been with

*tomorrow featuring me to be the past. The war for me
of which I thought was outwardly in regards of what I
did not have and the hardships some of those
circumstances brought always had me comparing what I
should be living like. The insecurities of what I didn't
have allowed me to build mental, physical, and spiritual
shields to aid me from further pain and defend me for
when I needed the most. From Humans, nature, and
energy by experiences, I know all occurred base on
reasoning, no such as chance, luck, or wish. You may
have an issue and have no clear idea on how to solve
but as you conclude your mind to quest for answer,
watch how the universe align those humans, nature,
and energy to correlate you in an understanding. Since I
was in my early teenage years, my normal abilities to
breathe was deficient, something I would never know
but find ways to manipulate. I did but never was I
educated, I learned mostly from doing then finding out
what happens when you do rather then being explained
the options before you do. I suffer from hyoid bone
syndrome, what is this to be exact, an horror film living
inside of me. The causes to my effect is explained by
trauma, anxiety, depression, restless, stressful
situations. So what exactly precipitated this issue when
the effects was an lifestyle I knew nothing about or I had
no idea was wrong for me. Maybe it could of been that
traumatic painful situation that left me toothless in
Ayiti, the family molestation, the abuse from my birth
giver, the absence of no parents, poor diet, and etc. I
have no answer or an precise moment but I am the
saying "Lucky", I am 1 out of 11 million who may have
suffer from this hyoid bone syndrome. In the past 15*

years, there's only been two or three surgery where the neck would be open to connect loose soft bone carthlidge that's not align correctly leaving an 10 inch scar going down the middle of the neck. How else may I defeat this matter, only threw nature. Frustrated as can be, our breathe and vocals is like the chakra alignment steering from the bottom of our stomachs, going up to the bottom of our jaws. In this effect, the hyoid bone syndrome is the middle ground of inhaling and exhaling. Issues of clarity in speech, being out breath, clogged air threshold are the daily norms of this factor. Being that this is my cause, you sometimes feel as you cannot breathe so holding my breathe and meditating like a monk was a norm for me in the art of manipulation or mentally diffusing pain I visually seen going away. Calisthenics became a go to as my neck, back, hips, legs are all effected by my body misalignment. The body is like an motor vehicle, you get what you put in and also if one piece is not in place, the effect it can have on the other pieces can be more damages down the line. My calling thru artistry prevails me as I'm unlimited too what I can achieve. Your abilities is not up too others but again is upon you, all that can become true is only up too you and the things that you do in actions you are attentive to do. Nothing from yesterday should limit how I live in today. My story is not my story but our story. How we all start don't define how we end, be fruitful, the seed of truthful to begin........9

MOETRY

~ Misty lady, set my spirit
free........?

In nature, my body is wind,
flowing across seas, amongst the
stars.

Global connection, 360 I spin,
glowing amongst darkness,
Polarity Bass sections threw bars.

~ Desires?........

Power or weakness can be
obtained,

The strength of polarity, decisions
one must maintain.

What is good threw the eyes of bad
!?,

We front in the act of happiness,
back behind is sad.

Anger, my desires I leave in the
moment of lust,

"what a man got to do",
determination in must.

Must thy be better then the
experience of yesterday,

Life courses means change, I usher
the differences my way.

My path, to respect life and what
is given to me,

Comprehension of Love, joy,
freedom, the feelings that my eyes
can see.

Stuck defines the pattern of an
continuous behavior,

Knowledge brings wisdom,
understanding you find in
nature.

Desires I have non, Will Power,
thy shine Sun.

~ 1 CELF 1........?

No need for anger,

Just an parliament of life which
sums up danger.

Live to enjoy and forgive,

Killing is an repercussion which
destroys rather then too love.

Been there - done that, Life's idea
of experience,

Shopping for chakras threw a low
life brings the value of clearance.

Know your worth and deny the
one' which defines you,

For all that can be accomplished
can be sustained threw.

Hard work - More Like smart
thinking,

A second of trust can be the
change quicker than a blinking,

Drinking threw the fountain of
youth, mind up float while the
body sinking.

Above Aqua is celf mission
although liquid flows current,

Blood in water, my cuts deep yet
never seen an surgent.

Inhaling for the power of breathe,

Exhale right whether drawn too
middle or left.

~ Celf Love + World Love = Best Love?........

I do for oneness.

The things I can control, my positions, my role,

The road ahead signs, fee required to ride life toll.

Model citizen, societal line created as an walking path,

Grading us from ethnicity, gender, success, human scores given as math.

I rather not, live for others rather then for the love of me,

The doings are my choices to what
I ought to be.

Clocking in, clocking out, factory
Humans threw assembly,

An locked up Elephant, strong
body but a weak mind tendency.

Caring for views, impressionable
thoughts of celf worth,

Insecurities runs canals darker
then the beginning as birth.

Some places, I see, feel but never
been,

Traveler of time, I'm the becometh
of air too wind.

Hidden talent, How can I do for celf which transcends you ?,

Dual skillset, I aim to bring oneness between separation that makes two,

So True.

Secrets........?

With this killing inside,

I'm lost in my world with no map to guide.

Compulsively, too mycelf, I lies, I'm okay!,

"doesn't matter", inner emotions of my say.

"Know one cares", Lost soul thinks why share,

Gutting out truths becomes a falsely dare.

On trial, tribulations I explain,

Justified wrongs for all one maintain.

Confidence makes the man,

"A baby got to do", An Rugrat
motto plan.

Think again, are my actions
tellable,

Saying is one thing but am I
doing the capable,

Take a shot, it is makeable.

Share yourcelf, you're not lost as
you may perceive,

Iron sharpens Iron, threw one
fountain we achieve.

Close trial, don't live too hide,
Open secrets, don't die with pride.
~ Nine. Twenty-six. Eight?........

Great, say,

Anointed, this is thy day.

Grateful, what I sustain made
humble,

My heart in hand, a grip I cannot
fumble.

Moments in the now, never
content nor prudent,

Daily sessions of how made me a
life long student.

Crlf joy must be shown,

Audio in ocean, Bass rhythmic
tone.

I am the greatest, mind version of
the body celf,

Threw thy spirit, I livid for my
health and wealth.

I will never be zero days old again,

Celf refinement, its my Birth
date, daily I win.

~ Mi Backbone........?

I stand strong understanding your
fear,

Protective, there's no wrong as you
being my rear.

Sincerely, I start with appreciation too you as dearly,

What I front is not my back views I feel as clearly.

Thrice born, thrice scorn, mi life threw a trilogy,

In my efforts, hard to find, my quest was serendipity.

My body is a planet, In spirit I'm universe,

In conscious a slave, inherited mi father's curse,

Battling the demons which were stuffed in mi mothers purse.

Still I rise, daily having you too
fall on,

Never alone, I stand strong

I love you, celf letter too mi
backbone.

~ Push, Shove is on the
way?........

I just wanna express !, Whatever is your action, is this truly success !?.

Seemingly I must live out the grid threw the body in prayers too be bless.

Drained I'm tired, noisy surroundings scattered like loosed wires,

Living flatten, A life with no purpose is just a car with no tires.

Knowing my worth annoys me, cant fit in, cant do what seen all do,

False reasonings gives out difference like they're all true.

Ignorance is an bliss,

Some defines the truth by a
mirrors mist.

Frustrating, celf questions why
am I here,

Internally afraid of mycelf,
externally I am my fear.

I'm close too mi heart but so far
from my purpose,

Many pain from the start, a love
dwelled threw the curses.

Silence been my power, Actions
are my wisdom,

Nurturing my hours from the
understanding of freedom.

A breathe can take you at ease,

A note to Bass, "Don't give up
Please"

~ Stop - Pacing - Go - Full - Need
- Speed - Racing - Indeed........?

Lost too many thoughts threw
time,

Repetition of word play I must
say, threw rhymes.

Contents, most don't live threw
but read as his story,

Whatever's the unknown, most
search outward like unsolved
mystery.

My only hate, the things I should
control,

Society gave me part, Never did I
request such role.

Just to start, most died in dreams
for money,

Paper trails, written context of
scummy.

Disrespectful, how we treat our
cells threw celf,

Ignorant too our mess,
materialisms gravitate if thou
wealth.

I'm steady late working for an
system that inflicts me with
hate,

Never good enough, "The Man's"
far distance perception of great.

Internally, I know everything
but all,

In all is all like a shadow of an
midget appearing tall.

Goal going for mines, celf trust is a
must indeed,

Time's a race, rolling my space,
outer thy speed achieved.

~Xtra Salti Iz D Suga
Honi?........

Jump into my bag, no definition
enters but versatility,

Plain in sight, cuffed diamonds,
I'm pressured jewelry.

Priceless writing, less priced
action,

Meaning for satisfaction, less is
done without passion.

In fabrication, I've been waiting,
virtue of time,

An Lemon squeeze though could
never be ripe as lime.

One day is someday, in today I
chooses route like a one way,

Modeling celf, I've been
visualizing podium runway.

You cannot forgive what you
cannot forget,

In retrospect, these the doings of
neglect.

With An lotus focus, inspired to be
what never not to be,

Thrice born, dual scorn, three
means trilogy.

In vice versa, thy so bad, Bass
makes good take a kneel,

Frozen flag, even force wind feels
Bass inner chill.

Seek balance threw the
treatment of unequal,

Weaponry mind, my spirit is
lethal.

An fighter with no sword, wireless connection but still cord.

Baked Applause comes in rounds like a toast,

Came from sightseeing towns to becoming the host.

I suggest, stay up on life, your progression,

Dedication, Literature truths, Levitation by my lessons.

~ The voyage........?

The energy of negative is positive
one's ahead,

I rather die living young then to
livid old and dead.

Socialism, always testing a
ninja,

You're not good enough, you don't
deserve, stressing a Ninja.

A ninja, when opportunity
knocks, I answer to become,

Celf hate is an repetitive gain
that keeps you where your from.

Should I wait or go ?, Virtue of
patience or anticipation !,

There's always an verdict answers
& questions breeds communication.

Fuse fueled, I'm iron turned too
fire,

Inside my abilities, Cosmo
connected as wire.

Threw this connection, Evil dwells
on my gains,

Seeing my care, hearing my Love,
obstructing me pains.

Could this be, due to lack of
believe, wish, or putting hope on a
pray,

My faith is loss, no religions which
governs, Spirituality my way.

My source is all, controlling any
and many of everything,

An start to an end, 360,
unification of an ring.

Positive is me, the spirit within,

Negative my lies, a friend of
pretend.

My compass, my boat cruise to mi
happen,

Smooth sailing, celf awareness,
Celf captain.

~ *Cheri-Mwen / Se-Lavi?........*

Mi two Angels, created by an
Goddess, Life's a Queen, no modest.

Miss Mother nature, the season
changes,

9 months the seeds implanted, you
birth in ranges.

Far, beyond to what's captive to
an Man imagination,

I thank life, in you life, birth the
youths too mi nation.

I'm procreation, too my seeds of
daughters, my life brings,

The harmony of celf respect
rhythm my tones, thy heart sings.

For my all, Lady's, I live to
provide,

Foundation for love, wisdom, my
understanding as guide.

The truths, rather not decept you
from life and hide,

Your true powers wont be find
outer but what stands in you
firmly inside.

I'm not or ever be the perfect man
but my love I test you to
challenge,

The darkness of past, seed my future, in presence I balance.

I've been loving you my seeds and Goddess garden long before manifestation,

My lady's been my thoughts governing my universe, set proclamation.

I came from no love, learning to know love,

Above hate love is great love, at your best, you're all my love.

~ Kemitry........?

The best love is one that I can feel,

Like wind on an open scar,
reflection, in time thy heal.

No medicine can adhere the pain
of reality,

Lust drugs, floatation of illusions,
my leaves gravity.

Seeing my visions in moments
alone,

Living an life of succession, no
soul shall condone,

Exerted my body living on Earth,
so brainless my home.

Up in space flow, fighting
separation of the body, in mind I
let go,

Success, defined under polarity,
humanity seeks Yes - No.

Learning from the phases giving
by the power of wisdom,

Trilogy my body, mind, soul that
enchants my inner kingdom,

Shh, in silence hear freedom.

Alchemy, the recipe I've gather for
the taste in life,

Air, Water, Fire, Earth, My
devoted wife, birth giving thrice.

~ Yang back Ying?........

Learning to gain in a fight with
maintain,

Running threw pain is the life
I've obtain.

Drained, mentally the flesh of my body disagrees spiritually,

Eternally, I know more than I wanted too, harmful memory.

Don't wanna recall the times out the body, physic withdraw,

Unorthodox, I see what's right yet defend southpaw.

I view fear blind sided by bravery,

Growths sense smell rooted by tendency.

Polarity is the battle, once one knows such exist,

One sided mist is truly an dual bliss.

A kiss, I send out too the rainbow,

Chakra align, my tears are
strength form just as the rain
flow.

~ Twinning........?

How many times I felt you with
us both knowing !, fantasies
unexplained.

Can't wait to see the hesitation
your body present jerking
backward as I enter forward
inside.

Open wide, I'm liable to stretch
your universe, show me your spirit
threw good and worse.

My strokes, your ocean, our boat,
we rocking,

My boots, your door, shake loose,
we knocking.

Which I can write your name,
you don't know my name and
you're still an secret.

In me, I'll keep this love safe
until eternity calls for change,

No matter the circumstances,
your love always in range.

Affirmation, I aim too attract
any law which obstruct me
towards you,

Met you by spirit, in physic, a
mental rendezvous.

Louder than words are actions,

Seeing is believing, doing is the
coming of attraction.

I'm come in, prepare too be mother,

Manifestation of the present, the
seed of an father.

Don't lend me your heart if I must
return as borrow,

Give me all or nothing and please
forsaken your sorrow.

In need, Indeed, I feel you

Thy light, blossoming over your
garden, A pedal I rose too.

Your moon shines my Sun,

Your Sun Dims my Moon.

~ It's okay 2 grow?........

water bounds fall, I'm shorter
than tall,

In fact, I'm most too all,

In act, I'm stand before crawl.

Known as thy too yawl, related
as connection comes call,

The master of Law, the judger of
flaw.

Height, the perception of lies,

Low, the tearing notions of cries.

Slicing up apple for the baking of
pie,

Life is not chances, either you
cause it or die.

I wonder !?, Most say why try ?,

Perceptional lie, gender
assumptions is only woman and
guy.

What goes up, is an must to calm
down,

Reversed role, a slave kinging
with an crown.

Water baby, Suffocating belly
hate made me nearly drown,

Ounces of pain begone my celf
loving by the pounds.

Gained balance, the key to my
life,

Duality unified like husband too
wife.

~ 2B or not 2B........?

Be truthful or die with a heavy
heart,

Be fruitful, a roots end to the very
start.

Can't live off, how you want me
too,

Can't give life, my being to do.

Powers I know, I must sustain,

Knowing my weakness, non cant
remain.

My futures my past, brightness of
darkness,

Past is my present, Loving in
likeness.

Then the change gonna come,

Die for an difference until this
pains me numb.

Made up my mind, living for
Love,

Acted on the hate, effects I should
of put above.

Higher, breaking ceilings as my
feet leaves ground floor,

Untamed, unlocked, finally
received key's to Pandora's door.

Deep in my core, I store.

Perfection, distant long ways
from neglection.

This ends my confessions,

Celf insured, Celf Progression.

~Outer religions covers inner
Spiritual pyramids?........

I'm asking more for the
understanding of faith,

Struck no believes, impatient,
can't wait.

Days changes though yesterday
ways the same,

A man's viewpoint can't be my
picture to frame.

Word is bond. As causes by actions,

Life is math, you add it,
multiply, divide some losses as
subtraction.

Don't tell me a name,
descriptively called GOD,

God, Oil, & drugs yet religions the
odd.

Every clan believes they're the
chosen ones,

So special a birth, mothers gifts
daughter's and son's.

We got so many name for this life
!,

Was Adam fornicating Eve
without making her his wife !?,

Sharpener, no pencil, mental tool
see's spirit as knife.

Cutting and slicing, invading the curses, I came out the vices,

A roller my gamble is the chance taking, remembering a throw provides numbers in dices.

How so many expect you to walk a straight line without questioning the blue or red pill,

Heard the devil runs the church, repenting all sins yet is such sent too hell still.

The womb of our world is infested, thrusted adversity,

Birthing religion to read out as nursery.

Hear no evil, se no evil,

Humans means people, different
Gods changes equal.

~ Peeled Layers........?

Have you ever thought of an
thought !, that in thoughts made
you thought, a lot of thoughts
about the first prior thought !?.

Thoughts.

Here to give or be taken, infant
sense, candy from a baby,

Can lead the driven of misleading,
unknown identity, transgender
lady.

Then in maybe can chances be
possible,

The bristle of boars brushing out
follicle.

Thought able, any wonder what is
brushing my hair or why is
animal clothe able !?,

Paper roots a tree but if add fire,
all becomes burnable.

Can't complain I'm still
breathing though Loss many
rounds, fighter anatomy, 1 round
in all is capable,

How can you laugh threw such pain but in rain comes joy like animation, life graphics all comical.

Just because you think it, does not mean you have to say it,

Just because you done t, does not mean you have to spray it.

The tongues loose but the minds control it,

Spirit Buddha, Peace in mind, condone it.

1 Love

2 Unifies

3 Visualize

4 Multiplies

5 Degrees

6 Negatives

7 Laws

8 Births

9 Plants

Bassary ~ celf terminologies

9 = Highest numerical universal digit. Sacred universal Love powered by Wisdom, Unity and understanding. The infinite energy of mathematics by

addition, subtraction, division, multiplication and nature

Bass = Beneficiate All Sounds Soulfully. To be.

Beneficiate = too apply credentials of the will set within your soul from your actionable mindset. In all doings, setting positive energies in all beings.

Birth giver = An impregnated wombman by sacred energy xchange with an Human male or "mental, spiritual manifestation" who then gives birth but did not raise her womb spiritually, consciously or physically.

Brotha = Melanin urban American dialect of an male by sibling's or ancestral relations.

Celf = the description of self and life cells implemented as one, to be all in the phases of one. Unifying your mind, body and spirit

Kaizen = "continuous improvement". Growth and education in every process of life. To never be stagnant, remaining rooted and blossoming fruitfully.

Kemitry = Kemit, origin name meaning the Black Land, original name known for current location as Egypt. Known also to be the founder of Alchemist teachers and students, known today as Scientist. The study of matter from people, places, and nature and the content which can be created by the mixture of

nature givings as Air, water, Fire,
Soil, etc.

Lavi = Creole translation of life.

MAKTUB = "It is written". To be
confirmed, the future is set in the
presence. Nothings a chance, all
was to suppose to happen which
has happen

Moetry = Artistic literature birth
govern by Poetry and Motion
unified too create as one.

Pyrrhic = "successful with heavy losses". "The battle we may lost, the war we win together". To not be counted by defeat but perseverance.

Seed giver = An human male encountering one or multiple wombman threw sacred energy xchange who then creates life with and does not raise his seeds spiritually, consciously or physically.

Sacred Energy Xchange = full
terminology for the acronym
known as S.E.X.,. The fluid
exchange of the male and female
body parts of an penis and vagina.
The mental, spiritual, and
physical temperament created in
this oneness can unify or separate.
The understanding of life
creations.

Sista = Melanin urban American
dialect of an wombman by
sibling's or ancestral relations.

Wombman = The human life carrier, the goddess of humanity. Nature's calling by cycle and seasons. The true living deity of higher powers.

Specials thanks too every
encounter, negative and positive.
Grateful for every experience,
regardless if I warranted or not,
this made me ~ JaMes PeTer
BasTiEN

Made in the USA
Columbia, SC
02 January 2020

86091696R00083